THE HARM

MR. PALMER: A ninety-year-old vegetarian nudist who spends his days swimming laps.

MONA: A would-be actress who plays aspirin tablets and giant ants in TV commercials.

TESS: Mona's highly charged film-maker daughter who carries a camcorder everywhere, film-ing the story of her life—which may include a few scenes with Gabriel.

CASSANDRA: The resident roller-blading psychic, whose predictions are only slightly off-target.

Join Gabriel, his Dad and Timmy the Otter for an adventure in living life on the "wild side"!

Other Avon Flare Books by
Ron Koertge

THE ARIZONA KID
THE BOY IN THE MOON
MARIPOSA BLUES
WHERE THE KISSING NEVER STOPS

THE HARMONY ARMS

RON KOERTGE

AN AVON FLARE BOOK

The characters and events in this book are fictitious. Any similarity to real persons, living or dead, is coincidental and not intended by the author.

AVON BOOKS
A division of
The Hearst Corporation
1350 Avenue of the Americas
New York, New York 10019

First Avon Flare Printing: September 1994

AVON FLARE TRADEMARK REG. U.S. PAT. OFF. AND IN OTHER COUNTRIES, MARCA REGISTRADA, HECHO EN U.S.A.

Printed in the U.S.A.

RA 10 9 8 7 6 5 4 3 2 1

For my wife, Bianca Richards,
& for my agent, Bill Reiss

Thanks to the students I met at Topeka West High School for their 1990 Author's Day, who walked me through this book when it was barely more than an idea.

Thanks also to the National Endowment for the Arts. Part of the time and money afforded by my 1990 fellowship in poetry enabled me to finish this book.

THE HARMONY ARMS

Gabriel's father used his index finger to sweep up all the crumbs on the shiny but battered pizza tray. Then he picked at the tiny pile.

"Go ahead and eat the last piece," Gabriel said.

Sumner patted his round stomach and shook his head. His pale hair moved slowly, as if he were underwater.

"For you. Your mom said you don't eat enough."

"I eat plenty." He shoved the huge pie pan back across Pizza Shack's wooden table. "I don't have to overload on carbs just to get on a plane to L.A."

Sumner spun the plate around, then urged the giant slice of pepperoni at his son. He used both hands, sinking almost all of his fingers into the thick cheese. He closed his eyes and acted like he was using the marker on a Ouija board.

"G," he intoned, trying to sound spooky over the crash and ping of nearby video games. "A." The pointy slice turned this way and that. "B."

Sumner was getting into it, rolling his head and stiffening both arms as if the spirit of the Ouija-pizza had taken over his whole body.

Embarrassed, Gabriel snatched the last slice, stuffed half of it into his mouth, and sank into a corner of the booth.

"I'm eating, okay? Look."

Sumner licked each finger lovingly. "It was spelling your name."

"Right, Dad." He took a drink of Coke and wiped his mouth.

His father patted his seersucker sport coat as though he were looking for a wallet or keys. Then he turned around and scanned the room.

"Dad?"

Sumner stood up. He pulled Timmy out of his pocket.

"Dad! Please!"

Too late. He was halfway across the room, the hand puppet tucked behind his back so the kids he was heading for couldn't see it.

Gabriel watched him get down on his knees in the sawdust. He saw Timmy play peekaboo over the edge of the table, then grab for Sheila's Coke as the little girl shrieked, a sharp squeal of pleasure picked up by other little kids as they spotted Timmy and tried to squeeze past their parents.

Gabriel put his Cardinals baseball cap on and pulled it low over both eyes. He knew people were staring at his dad. He didn't want to see the fathers of the second-graders Sumner taught smile until he moved on, then roll their eyes at their wives.

"What's happening, bro?"

Gabriel nodded at Mark Blocker, a kid in his class and the catcher on his ball team. Then they both looked at Sumner.

"Your old man is something else," Mark said.

Gabriel squirmed. "Yeah, but what else? That's what I can't figure out."

4

Across the room, Sumner took Timmy's hand and began to waltz.

"Probably he'll settle down in L.A.," Mark said.

"Don't bet on it."

"Maybe you could stay with us. It's just for a month, right?"

Just then somebody shouted, "For God's sake, Sumner. Look what you've done! That puppet of yours is shedding."

Mr. Davis, vice-principal of the middle school Gabriel went to, was picking polyester fur out of his wife's salad.

"Oh, man," Gabriel groaned, shoving Mark out of the way.

Outside, breathing hard from his sprint through the restaurant, Gabriel tried to collect himself. He looked around at his hometown, picking out landmarks and concentrating on them, doing what his mother had advised, which was to stop thinking and imagining and worrying and just be in the present. What she called The Now.

There were the streets of Bradleyville, straight and narrow. Mr. Tarrant was just closing up the gun shop, pulling the heavy screen across the already-locked doors, then locking it. Plastered across the windows of Video Row were Arnold Schwarzenegger posters. And somebody was sweeping the sidewalk in front of Manchester's Cleaners, really sweeping hard like anything soiled had better watch out.

"Hey!" piped Timmy in his ear.

Gabriel twisted away, but the sleek brown head with its button eyes and stiff acrylic whiskers followed him.

"Dad! I have asked you a million times to not talk to me with that dumb puppet."

Sumner hid Timmy behind his back. "You used to like it," he said in his usual soft voice.

"So what! I used to sleep in pajamas that had feet in them."

Timmy looked down at the ground, acting penitent. Sumner looked down, too. When he made a line in the gravel with his shoe, the puppet's eyes followed the scuffed Hush Puppy back and forth.

"I think L.A.'s going to be different," Sumner said finally.

Gabriel rolled his eyes. "Good guess, Dad."

"I mean for me. For us. Even *I'm* not going to be able to sit around a table with a bunch of hotshot writers and talk like an otter."

Timmy rose from his side and stared at him, whiskers twitching.

"Well, you can come," Sumner said to his hand, "because if it weren't for you, we wouldn't even be going to California. You just can't talk all the time."

Then the puppet turned and gazed at Gabriel, opening his white-tipped paws.

"He wants a hug," Sumner said. "He thinks you're mad."

Gabriel plunged his fists deep into the cargo pockets of his jeans.

"I'm not hugging that puppet," he said deliberately, "because as far as I'm concerned there isn't any puppet, okay? Nothing to hug, nothing to talk to, get it?" He followed his father's gaze. "Now what?"

Twenty yards away, his mom and Warren were locking their sleek bicycles.

Sumner folded Timmy carefully. "That guy really bugs me," he said, glaring at Warren, who was dressed in black tights with a white top and looked like a trendy salt shaker. "He passes me on that bike all the time. And *I'm* in the Subaru, so I have to look at his behind for about ten miles."

"Just stand up straight," Gabriel urged. "You're taller than he is."

When Gabriel's mom spotted them, she touched Warren's arm and headed their way. She wore a biking outfit the color of summer fruit—persimmon, peach, and plum. Her heelless shoes clicked as she walked.

Warren took his helmet off and shook his headful of curls, but Alison left hers on. It was shaped like a huge windswept tear. She looked like somebody on *Star Trek*.

"How was the pizza?" Warren asked, too cheerfully.

"Round," Gabriel replied. Then he looked at his father. "We have to go, right, Dad?"

"Sure." Then he added, "Where?"

Alison smiled, tugging at one stained glove. "Plane's Wednesday, right? Eight-thirty?"

Sumner nodded.

"Don't forget," she admonished, "to set the alarm in Gabriel's room, too. He'll never wake up on his own."

"Did I ever miss the school bus once?" Gabriel demanded.

"I woke you up."

"Not every day you didn't."

She looked at Sumner and mouthed, "Set the alarm."

Warren tried again: "I heard about your good luck, Sumner. Congratulations."

Sumner reached for his pocket, but Gabriel slapped at his hand.

"We'll see," Sumner mumbled.

Alison shifted her weight so that she stood a little crooked, then made her grin crooked, too.

"What's it mean that we're married for thirteen years and you make twenty-seven thousand a year, and then as soon as we get divorced, Hollywood starts calling?"

Sumner's hand floated toward his pocket; then he caught Gabriel's eye.

"I don't know," he said, looking at the ground.

She patted his wrist. "Well, I hope it works out." Then she turned to her son, unsnapping the peculiar helmet and lateralling it deftly to Warren. Looping one arm around Gabriel's shoulders, she turned him away from the others as she tried to coax a smile out of him.

"You promised you wouldn't be a grouch, remember?"

"Mom," he whispered intently, "I can't do this. I can't spend a month alone with him and that otter."

"You won't be alone, Gabriel. There are people at the apartment complex, that Harmony Arms place."

"But *you* won't be there."

"You chose not to come with me."

Gabriel scowled. "That was like picking between hot beets and cold beets. I can either ride a bicycle around the world with you and your boyfriend"—he held up one finger—"or"—he held up another—"I can go to L.A. with Dad and *his* boyfriend, who is a lot shorter than Warren but only a little hairier."

"I think it's important that you spend some time alone with your father."

"But all my friends are here!"

She smoothed his hair. "Honey, you'll make new friends."

He snuck a look at his father, who was standing stiffly by Warren, both arms wrapped around himself as if he were cold.

"I can't break in new friends in a few weeks, not once they get a load of him." He began to plead with his mother: "I could stay with Mark. He said so."

"Gabriel, the Blockers live in a trailer."

"Well, alone, then. I'm old enough."

She shook her head. "Out of the question."

"What if I got a job and stayed at a motel or something? The team needs me!"

"Gabriel, you're going." She leaned to kiss him on the forehead. "This is for the best—believe me."

"But I already got my down-to-the-wire-champion-ship-Bradleyville-Badgers-haircut." He whipped off his baseball hat. His almost-blond hair had been cut close on the sides, then tapered up and leveled off with mathematical precision.

"I'm aware of that," she said dryly. "It'll grow out."

He tried one last time. "Mom, what if *you* were fourteen and he was *your* dad, how would you feel?"

Alison smiled. "I admit your father's not like everybody else."

"Tell me about it."

"But neither am I," she said firmly. "I want you to look around you when you get to Los Angeles." When Gabriel acted exasperated, she added, "I don't mean at things. I mean at the people, what they do and why they do it. It's not going to be like Bradleyville. Thank God." She pushed some damp hair back. "I'll bet everyone will be different. I *hope* they will be, and I hope that'll be okay with you." She reached for his chin and nudged it up. "Will you do that for me?"

"I still don't see why I have to. . . ."

Suddenly Alison put her damp forehead against her son's dry one.

"You know, I like this bike riding stuff. For now, anyway. I like feeling strong, and I like being competitive. But if I didn't think it was best and if I felt you were going to be really, really unhappy, I wouldn't go. But it is best. Trust me."

Gabriel took a breath before he said, "Okay, I guess. But when school starts, I live with you again, right? Like before."

Arm in arm, they turned back to the others.

"I know we covered this, Sumner," she said, "but remember—when you get there, tell my machine your number. I'll call from wherever we are." She glanced at Warren. "Probably Durango?"

"Probably. There's a shorter race in Memphis, though, so . . ."

She looked from father to son. "Anyway, we'll work it out so nobody has to worry about anybody, okay?"

As the quartet awkwardly said their good-byes, Warren added heartily, "Maybe we'll all go next year."

"I'm not going anywhere on a bicycle," Timmy piped. "I hate dry land."

They all looked at Sumner's squirming pocket.

Gabriel tugged at his dad's arm. "We gotta go."

▼ ▼ ▼

Three days later, when Gabriel and Sumner stopped in the shade just inside the courtyard of the Harmony Arms Apartments in Burbank, California, Gabriel tried to stand just far enough away so that people might think they weren't together, that it was a coincidence they'd walked in off the street at just about the same time. Because not only was Timmy out, glancing every which way, but Sumner's suitcase was one of those that has little built-in wheels and a leash, and Sumner had started to pretend that it was a dog named Roger.

"Not bad, huh, guys?" said Sumner, looking the place over. He tugged at the leash, and when the suitcase rolled forward, he said sternly, "Heel, Roger. Good boy."

Gabriel closed both eyes behind his sunglasses, the ones his dad had bought him at the airport. When he opened his eyes again, he was still in Los Angeles, staring at a squarish, two-story apartment complex either half built or half destroyed. There was lumber everywhere and some rickety-looking scaffolding. Most of the apartment's picture windows were divided into four panes like the windows on Christmas cards. But nearly all of them had huge taped X's, as if somebody had changed his mind about being merry. Some of the doors were boarded over.

A big hole had been gouged out of the ground right in the center of everything. Roots stuck out of the dry, flaky earth. Expensive-looking chaises—red, white, and blue like something at a resort for patriots—ringed the pit to keep anyone from falling in. But just beyond this was a long column of shimmering water, and someone was swimming. Regularly an arm rose above the deep blue tiles that lined the lap pool, moved through the air slowly like someone painting a ceiling, and then disappeared.

"I could sure use a dip," Timmy complained. "That flight dried my fur right out."

"Dad," Gabriel cautioned, "take it easy. Here comes somebody from the planet Earth."

A woman in gray Lycra stretch pants made her way toward them. She held one hand out, and the pink blouse she'd tied at the bottom rode up to reveal an inch or two of flat, very pale stomach.

"I'm Mona Miller," she said. "Obviously you found us."

"Sumner McKay," Gabriel's father said, holding out his only free hand. Then he pointed. "Plus Timmy, Roger, and Gabriel."

Mona smiled a little warily. "Gabriel and Timmy I know from the studio's paperwork, but Roger is new to me."

"I'm just playing," Sumner said. "Experimenting. I don't want to be a one-book author."

"Oh, I see. You're thinking of writing *Roger the Suitcase* next."

Just then Timmy swooped up and bit Sumner, locking his soft jaws to Sumner's cheeks. "Jealous," Sumner explained, making his left hand struggle with the right one as Mona laughed.

"Why don't you all come with me?" she said. "We'll go up to my office"—here she grimaced so it was clear she meant only a little table in the corner piled high with bills—"and I'll get you the keys and what-not."

"I'm okay here," murmured Gabriel.

As Mona studied him, he studied back, his jaw set.

Her even features were made a little blurry by freckles that swept downward from the bridge of her nose and out across both cheeks. Her hair was copper-colored in the angled afternoon sun, and her eyes—slate gray—reminded Gabriel of the color of blackboards on which had once been written riveting facts, important equations, or a poem.

"You look a little tired," she said. "At least take off your backpack."

"I'm all right."

"Well, then, I'll see if Tess won't come down and keep you company." And with that she led his father past the lap pool and up a flight of stairs.

When the door closed behind them and Gabriel thought he was alone, he sat down heavily, shrugged off the straps of his backpack, and hurled it at his dad's suitcase, knocking it over.

Then he leaned back warily onto one of the chaises. Above him the sky was the color of dirty milk and, floating in it, a Ritz cracker of a sun. Still it was hot, but not like in Bradleyville, where the sun drew the crops up out of the ground and coaxed petals out of flowers. This heat dropped out of the sky, ricocheted off the concrete, and zapped its way through every available forehead.

When he heard a door open and close, he turned. Someone—it was probably a woman, but she was wearing a blue baseball cap—had come out of one of the first-floor apartments and begun to skate. Both hands behind her back like Hans Brinker, she leaned into it, picking up speed, deftly weaving among the heaps of sand and piles of lumber. She didn't wear regular skates, but black roller-blades with neon green laces and matching wheels lined up one behind the other. A yellow muumuu flattened itself against her.

About halfway through the second lap, she slowed considerably, pitched forward with both hands on her knees, and glided toward Gabriel, head down. He read the *D* on the front of the blue wool cap and guessed Dodgers. Just underneath that, she had glued a deep red stone. Like a ruby, but the kind of ruby usually found in specially marked boxes of breakfast cereal.

She leaned to steady herself, then sprawled on a chaise catty-corner to Gabriel's. That's when he saw she was wearing a Dick Tracy muumuu, the yellow background decorated with the detective's sharp jaw and machine gun. Even from the back, Gabriel could see that her skin was like her muumuu—too big for her.

"What a workout!" she bragged to nobody in particular. Then she reached into a deep pocket, took out a can of beer, popped it open with a hiss, and drank at least half of it, the flesh along the underside of her arm swaying. "Time to unwind," she panted, "after a hard day of clairvoyance, astral travel, and deciphering the secrets of the tarot." Then she chuckled, finished the beer, dropped the empty can into another deep pocket, turned and asked, "So how's your mother, kiddo?"

Gabriel waited a second before he answered. He scanned the face and neck that had folded into themselves. Then he said quietly, "I don't know."

"Oh, my God." The woman half-stood for an instant. "I thought you were Tess. I apologize. I have got to go down to Thrifty's and get some glasses." She leaned toward Gabriel, squinting. Then she repeated, "Oh, my God," but more slowly. And with more reverence, so that it wasn't the mildest kind of swearing this time but a kind of prayer.

"What?" said Gabriel, annoyed.

"I can't believe it." She wiped at her eyes with one yellow sleeve and peered again. "I dreamed about you. I've *been* dreaming about you." Before he could stop her, she snatched one of his hands. The back of hers had liver spots the size of pennies and dimes. But it was warm and dry and strong. "You were flying, and you were flying here to Burbank to finish something."

"How can I finish anything? I just got here, and I don't know one person in the whole state."

"Wait a second." She squinted, then hit herself in the side of the head with the heel of one hand, like someone trying to get the TV to come back on. Then she shook her head and crowed. "But I saw it once—that's the point. I saw it just like I used to."

"This is Cassandra," said Mona, and Gabriel jumped, because he hadn't heard her or his dad come up behind him. "She's our resident psychic."

As Cassandra struggled to her feet, Mona pointed, "Sumner McKay, who's out here to work with some studio people. The little guy with the whiskers is Timmy the Otter, the big brown guy . . ."

"What happened to Roger?" asked Sumner, staring at the suitcase lying on its side. "He didn't get hit by a car, did he?"

Then Mona finished the list: "and Gabriel."

Cassandra held out her hand. "It would be Gabriel."

Then she gave her attention to Sumner, tilting her face up slightly, frowning with concentration, and rubbing his

soft hand between her thumb and forefinger like someone buying yard goods.

"Artistic," she murmured, "definitely artistic. And sensitive. A deep, deep sensitivity. Do I see colors *and*
words, or just—"

"Both," Sumner interjected. "I illustrate my own
books."

"Exactly! Yes, and your success will stem from that."

"Really? I'll be successful?"

"Oh, yes. Very. But"—just like that her expression
changed, darkened, like drawing venetian blinds shut—
"I feel conflict, too. Not so much physical conflict as
emotional, though it could be partly physical, I guess, I
mean . . ."

Immediately, Timmy darted toward Cassandra. "I'm
next. Read my paw, please," he squeaked.

Cassandra grinned, showing all five teeth, the three
beige ones and the two that had turned completely
brown. Then she took Timmy's paw—the one made by
Sumner's thumb—and peered at it intently.

"I see deep pools," she said. "Clear, cool water and
clams that open themselves up when they see you coming."

"What a wonderful future," said Sumner as Timmy
clapped his brown paws soundlessly. "Now do Gabriel's."

Gabriel locked both hands behind his back and retreated a step or two.

"No, thanks. I mean it, okay?"

Mona took Sumner's arm then and moved toward the
other stairs, the ones that began near the palm tree by
the entrance. "Why don't I show you two where you're
going to be living?"

Sumner got Roger on all fours and dusted him off, then followed Mona. As Gabriel reached for his backpack, Cassandra said, "If you change your mind, come by anytime. The future's always at home."

It was the way the sun caught the ruby on her blue hat that held Gabriel, fixed him there for an instant. Or longer, actually. Until Mona called to him and he jogged across the concrete and the artificial grass, shaking his head like he'd dozed off.

Mona and Sumner waited for him at the top of the stairs. He could tell they were talking, so he slowed his climb, then stopped a step or two from the landing and stared out across the U-shaped court. From the second story he could see the swimming pool was shaped, of all things, like a Valentine, but only the shallow, pointy end was paved. The lone swimmer in the lap pool continued, his arms rising and falling so slowly he seemed to be only holding his own against some invisible current.

As Mona turned to point, her voice got louder. "I know the builder, and his vision, as we say in Los Angeles, was lots of young women with silicone in everything but their eyebrows lounging by his cardiac-shaped pool while hot young producers cut deals in the fitness center. Instead, right after almost all the old-timers had moved out so the builders could come in, the recession hit. Your place is the only condominium he ever finished." Mona gazed across the deserted courtyard and rubbed her arms as if she were cold. "Frankly, it'll be nice to have a man around again. It's eerie sometimes."

"A man and an otter!" squeaked Timmy as Gabriel looked at his shoes.

Mona smiled as she leaned toward Gabriel. "By the

way, I'm almost always home, so I never want you to feel like you're alone."

"I'm sort of used to being alone. Part of the time, anyway."

"I'm dreading the day, though," she said, "when something happens and the old Harmony Arms actually becomes the Isle of Eden, or the whole place gets torn down so they can put up a Hypermarket. I don't exactly know what Tess and I will do, much less Cassandra and Mr. Palmer."

"I'll be making all kinds of money pretty soon," Sumner interjected. "So if you ever need any . . ."

Mona laughed and shook her head so hard her hair swished around her face. She reached for Gabriel then, letting her hand rest on the back of his neck. "Promise me," she said, "you won't let your dad talk to anybody who has a Rolex for sale or who leases a Porsche, okay?"

Gabriel only nodded, because he would've had a hard time saying anything. It was the way she'd touched him. How his mom had touched his hair at the airport in St. Louis.

Mona led them down a long, partly carpeted hall, then paused outside 4B. "Ta-dah!" she said musically, and made a little ceremony of handing Sumner the keys. "And I want you to ask me for anything anytime, all right?" She turned to include Gabriel. "All right? The studio is paying me to take care of you guys, so it's not like you're imposing."

"Yes, ma'am."

"And ask Tess, too." Mona's eyebrows registered an expression of willing resignation. "However, my daughter the filmmaker sends her regrets today. She's editing."

18

Mona glanced around. "For right now, what if I help you carry in some things? These two bags can't be all your belongings."

"There are a few more things in the car," Sumner said, "but we can do it."

"So you have a car. Good."

"Yes. The studio Fed Ex-ed me the keys, and it was parked right where they said it would be."

"Which just proves that everybody in Hollywood is wrong, and studios do keep their promises." She flashed an encouraging smile. "What about food? This is Mother Hubbard's condo at the moment. Why not just leave your things inside, and I'll drive you to the market?"

"Maybe if you just pointed us in the right direction," Sumner said. "I'm inclined to strike out on my own with nothing but a compass and some dry matches." As Timmy rose from Sumner's side, he shrieked, "And a killer otter who guards the Harmony Arms!"

Gabriel cringed and snuck a glance at Mona, who, to his surprise, was smiling.

Twenty minutes later, as his dad carefully set the hand brake, Gabriel asked, "Leave you-know-what in the car, okay?"

Sumner got out and stared at his son across the shiny roof. "It's awfully hot. What if Timmy—"

"We'll crack a window!"

Sumner locked up carefully, peeked in, and waved good-bye. Then the two of them strolled across the spotless parking lot toward the entrance to Mrs. Maxwell's Ranch Market. They stopped to let a valet in a short red jacket help a bejeweled woman out of her silver sports car.

Gabriel tugged at his father's flowered shirtsleeve. "Maybe we'd better go to a regular store," he whispered.

"Why?"

"Are you kidding? They'll probably think I'm here to deliver potatoes." He pointed. "Look at these jeans."

"They look fine. They're brand new."

"Nobody else is wearing pants like this, and that woman who got out of the Porsche had on gold shoes!"

Sumner nudged Gabriel. A man dressed in green leather from head to toe glided by carrying a case of Evian water.

"Do you think he's a movie star?" Sumner whispered.

"Or a lizard." Gabriel started for the car. "Now, c'mon. Let's find us some place on a side street that just sells milk and bread and motor oil, like back home."

"Gabriel, my feet hurt, and I'm hungry. We'll just grab a few things and go back to the condo. What do you feel like—burgers? Why don't you get mustard and catsup and mayo, and I'll get everything else. We'll meet at the checkout stand."

Just inside the door was a coffee bar. Roasted beans were piled behind spotless glass. Gabriel watched his father inhale, his head thrown back with pleasure. Then Sumner spotted a nearby shelf of jams and jellies arranged from the lightest pineapple to the deepest berry.

"Look at this!" he shouted to no one in particular. Gabriel retreated into a flower-packed cranny and peeked out from behind a tiny potted palm.

"And wouldn't they be great on this?" Sumner announced, standing in front of the slanted glass of the bakery and gaping at the bread in loaves and twists.

Shoppers looked at him, angling their carts in the

other direction. One woman, thin as an exclamation point, clutched her purse with one hand and raised the other like a cleaver.

Head down, Gabriel scurried toward his father. "I don't think you're supposed to talk out loud in here, Dad. It's probably like a church. C'mon, let's stay together. I think the meat counter's this way."

They hurried past a live fish tank where women pointed fiery-tipped nails at the perfect lobster or trout. A few yards farther on, busy butchers in spotless white coats reached, wrapped, and said, "Thank you, ma'am," almost in unison.

Behind the thick glass, ground lamb had been molded into a sheep, pork became a huge pig's head with black olive eyes, and even the hamburger looked like a miniature cow.

As Sumner, smiling to himself, bent down for a closer look, Gabriel warned, "Don't start talking to those animals, Dad."

Sumner acted a little huffy. "I was just checking for freshness."

"Uh-huh. Well, check the prices. At six dollars a pound, we can't afford this stuff."

Sumner waved that away. "Let the new screenwriter worry about money. You find the condiments."

"Will you be okay?"

"I won't embarrass you, if that's what you mean."

Gabriel flinched, couldn't meet his dad's eyes, then turned away, dragging the cart. He stocked up a little, glancing at his father, who was chatting with the butcher and waving his hands. Then he leaned on the sturdy metal handle and scoped things out.

The kids who worked at Mrs. Maxwell's were amazing. Even their dumb straw hats and checkered shirts couldn't hide how great they looked. They must have all been class officers, cheerleaders, and water polo champions who worked because it was the cool thing to do, not because they had to.

Just then Sumner dropped the ground round into the cart, checked his son's purchases approvingly, and asked, "What did you think of that woman we met at the Harmony Arms, that Cassandra?"

"I don't know. Why?"

"Well, maybe she really is psychic. After all, she said I was sensitive."

"Sure, after Mona told her you were out here to work for a studio."

"So maybe I don't look like a stuntman. She still knew I was a writer."

"No, no. She said, 'Do I feel words or pictures or both?' And you said, 'Both,' and she said, 'Oh, yeah, right.'"

"So you didn't believe her when she told me I'd be successful?"

"Dad, what's she going to say, that there's a humiliating experience in store for you?"

"Hmm. I guess you're right." Then he stopped right beside a slender blond girl who was dusting bottles of wine. He reached down and rubbed at his foot before he asked, "Pardon me, Miss, but where are the Odor-Eaters?"

"Oh, God!" Gabriel groaned immediately, matching the color of the catsup.

The girl—her name tag said Lucinda—squinted thoughtfully. The tips of her feather duster caressed her flawless cheeks, reminding Gabriel that he had two new zits so red and huge they could have been used to signal low-flying aircraft. "Gosh," she said finally, "I just started here, so . . ."

"Just about anything by Dr. Scholl would do," Sumner assured her. "Foot powder, corn plasters . . ."

Lucinda brightened. "Oh, follow me," she said and then led them—Sumner limping, Gabriel pushing the cart with his head down as if it were heavy as a barge— straight to the produce section. She pointed to a bin of yellow corn, each ear shucked clean and lying beside its perfectly cloned neighbor.

"Here you go," she said.

Sumner began, "But—"

"It's fine!" Gabriel charged between them. He grabbed a paper bag. "These are perfect. Thank you very much." He started picking corn as fast as he could. "Just what we wanted. Bye."

When Lucinda had skipped away, Sumner put a restraining hand on his son's arm. "I'll go to the drugstore later. Let's put these back."

Gabriel clutched the brown bag. "I'll bet we have to buy them. I mean, I touched them already."

"Okay," Sumner said after a second. "Let's get out of here."

They made their way through half a dozen men who glided about in narrow leather shoes almost hidden by spotless cuffs. Their clothes hung luxuriously from their shoulders and hips. Sumner, though, looked rounder and softer than usual. He waddled a little as he walked. His clothes were, by contrast, nearly dangerous—the crease on his perma-pressed pants could have cut someone. And his huge shoes, planted into a V whenever he stopped, looked as big as badgers.

"It may be expensive, but I love this place," Sumner said, getting into line. And then to the man twice his age in the line beside his: "Isn't this a wonderful market?"

The old shopper's smile went on and off like Christmas lights.

"I like your shirt a lot," Sumner said then. "Where'd you get it?"

The man's eyes twitched. "Downtown," he replied softly but precisely.

Sumner grinned. "It's a little like mine."

Gabriel rolled his eyes. They were about as similar as chocolate cake and mud. The other man's shirt was ruby or salmon or rouge. Sumner's was red as a sore.

"C'mon, Dad. It's our turn."

Gabriel leaned into the cart and began to put things onto the spotless green conveyor at top speed. Sumner kept chatting with his new friend, who was looking around a little wildly.

A checker with the most beautiful eyes Gabriel had ever seen was running the cash register. She paused and looked at the huge bag on the scale, then at the digital price, which read $18.00, then at him.

"Are you on some kind of corn diet or something?"

Gabriel started to see all those little sparkly things that mean you're about to pass out. He took a couple of quick breaths, then put his head down and started for the door.

His dad called, "Gabriel?"

"I'm okay," he said, without turning or even looking around. "I just need some air. I'll meet you at the car."

▼ ▼ ▼

By the time Gabriel woke up the next morning, it was past ten. He remembered asking his dad to let him sleep, and he remembered mumbling good-bye to him a little later and being told to read the note on the kitchen table.

He wandered into the unfamiliar bathroom to pee, then stared in the mirror. One of yesterday's zits had pretty much disappeared, but another had sprung up all the way on the other side of his forehead. It was lined up perfectly with the remaining one, like two points in a geometry problem.

Gabriel was disgusted. "If Train A leaves Carbuncle Junction with a load of Clearasil at two o'clock . . ." He stared into his own eyes, brown like his mother's.

Standing on the kitchen table was a bowl, a spoon, and a new box of cornflakes. On its orange side, a football hero eluded an invisible opponent on his way to the goal line and a soft barrier of toothy cheerleaders. Gabriel, still in his underpants and T-shirt, moved a twenty-dollar bill to one side and picked up a longish note:

> *I let you sleep. I'm at the studio. (Phone number below.) Mona said her daughter, Tess, has to run an errand at noon or so and will drop by to see if you want to come along. You can call Mona anytime (phone number below) or go over. Have a good time! Relax. Take a dip. I'll call before lunch and say hi.*
>
> *Dad*

He toured the condominium again. The black leather furniture in the living room still smelled new; he sat down, patted it the way he might have patted one of the cows that roamed the wide pastures around Bradleyville, then bounced a little. By bending the white miniblinds on the big window in the living room, he could see the courtyard, deserted except for the same someone exercising in the long lap pool.

His father had made his own bed—just like back home—and he'd put everything away except for two hairbrushes. They crouched on the black lacquered dresser—gifts from his wife. Their ornate silver backs caught the overhead light. Between them stood a framed photograph of the three of them when they'd been a family. From the window nearby, he could see out across the neighborhood, which consisted of other apartments and condominiums. Lots of the smaller windows were covered with aluminum foil, and their reflected glare reminded Gabriel of the sunglasses Warren always wore.

The wallpaper in the hall was figured with silvery bamboo, and the carpet was deep green, so just wandering from one room to another was a little like a nature walk along a path hewn out of the forest. But the destination was never a waterfall or a view. Gabriel's room, in fact, looked out onto the almost deserted parking lot. And in the distance was a piece of freeway that arched, then dipped, then arched again like a mustache drawn across the face of the sky.

When the phone rang, he looked for it, then fumbled with the unfamiliar receiver, which didn't lie across the cradle like a normal phone but snapped in and out like a Dustbuster.

"Gabriel? It's Dad. Everything okay?"

"Uh-huh. I was just going to eat breakfast."

"It's great down here! We've got our own little office and everything. And the minute we get out of story conferences and onto a real set, I want you to come down here."

Gabriel rubbed his eyes. "Okay, Dad."

"So, did Mona come by yet? Or Tess?"

"No, I haven't been up very long."

"I know we talked about this, but I still feel a little guilty leaving you alone."

"I'm fine."

"You're not really alone, anyway. Mona's always home, remember? You should go over. You're not putting her out, really. She wants you to."

"Okay."

"Did you see the money on the table? Is it enough?"

Gabriel remembered the twenty. "It's plenty."

"Mona said Tess will show you the mall and the library and all that, okay?"

"Sure."

"I'll call you again this afternoon."

"Maybe not. If I'm out with this Tess character and can't answer the phone, you'll worry. So you just get some work done. Really, it's no big deal."

Sumner's voice dropped. "This guy down here, this Miles? He says *Timmy the Otter* could be *the* movie next summer. He's already talking about spin-offs for TV and all kinds of merchandising stuff—Timmy dolls and Timmy pajamas and I-don't-know-what-all."

"Great," Gabriel said without any enthusiasm because he was picturing himself finally turning sixteen and then getting a Timmymobile.

"Oh, and Gabriel? I just talked to your mother. She wanted to make sure we got in all right. She's going to call you any minute, okay?"

"Okay."

Gabriel had barely hung up when the phone rang again.

"Hi, Mom?" he said.

"Hi, sweetheart."

"Where are you?"

"At a pay phone in Colorado. We're . . . wait a minute, okay?" Gabriel shifted the receiver to his other ear. He knew she had one hand over the mouthpiece because it was like hearing through a pillow. "Warren, one more minute is not going to put you behind your precious schedule. Now, relax." Her voice got brighter. "Gabriel? How is it out there? Do you like it?"

"I've got my eyes open, like I promised." He pictured Cassandra skating down Main Street, right past the Methodist church. "And you were right. Already it's not like Bradleyville."

"Good. And you're fine?"

"So far, I guess. I'm going to hang out with some kid today." He didn't feel like telling her the kid was a girl.

"Well, be careful."

"All right."

"I gotta go. Warren's wringing his maps. I love you, okay?"

"Okay."

Gabriel got another glass of juice, then strolled into his bathroom and politely closed the door before he stripped and adjusted the water. Almost every time he took all of his clothes off, he felt sexy, which was a feeling he liked so much it made him uncomfortable.

As the water ran over him caressingly, Gabriel wondered if his dad thought about sex at all anymore. And even if his mom did, he would never ask; it made him kind of sick to his stomach to even think about it.

So he made the water chilly, finished up at top speed, then jumped into clean jeans and a T-shirt before merely being naked meant showtime in Gabriel's X-Rated Revue.

He'd just finished eating, just finished reading about star athletes and nutrition on the back of the cereal box, when there was a knock at the door.

"It's Tess!" someone—a girl—shouted. "Don't be afraid."

"Who's afraid?" Gabriel shouted back.

"You should be. This isn't BowWowville or wherever it is you're from. It's the city. And you don't have one of those peepholes in your door yet. But it's okay this time. Let me in."

When the door swung open, Gabriel looked right into the lens of a bulky camcorder, the kind daddies are always using to remember baby's every burp forever.

Tess peeked out at him from behind her eyepiece. "Close your mouth. You look like you were raised by sparrows."

Gabriel did, then swallowed, then backed away so Tess could come in, but she barked a "No!" at him as she began to narrate: "Interior. Day. A shabby apartment deep in L.A.'s mean streets. Bars of light fall symbolically across the acne-ridden face of young Elvis Miyata. Cut to background, where we see a rumpled bed and, tucked in, the bare shoulder and symbolically ash-blond hair of his sleeping paramour." Down came the camera. "Do you know what a paramour is?" she asked.

Gabriel shook his head slowly, taking in this girl. She was wiry and thin, a charged-looking thin, like a logo for the electric company. All topped by a midnight-in-the-graveyard haircut.

"It means girlfriend," she said.

"Then why not say *girlfriend?*"

She pointed to one ear. "'Cause *paramour* sounds better, and because it tells the director a lot. I mean, girlfriends do dishes, okay? Paramours never do."

Gabriel watched her take in the living room. Even her movements were quick and sharp, the way her elbows, nose, and knees were sharp. He couldn't imagine her simply sitting down, but lighting someplace instead. Poised on the surface of the world.

She held out one hand. "Tess Miller."

"Gabriel McKay." Her hand was warm—not as warm as Cassandra's maybe, but pretty warm.

"Gabriel in the City of the Angels," she said with a grin. "Kind of redundant, isn't it? Do you know what *redundant* means?"

"Yes. Or should I say, 'Yes, yes'?"

Tess laughed soundlessly, licked her finger, and chalked one up for Gabriel. "You ready?"

"I guess. I sure don't want to just hang around here all day." He patted his pockets and found the new key.

"Shoot me first, okay?"

Gabriel stared. He'd heard L.A. was violent, but . . .

Tess swung her black camcorder into position, holding it by the handle with a niche for every finger. "With this."

"I knew what you meant."

Tess stepped behind him, balanced the camera on one shoulder, guided his fingers, and tapped the eyepiece. "Don't worry about doing it right."

Gabriel squinted. "Just, what, keep you in this little square?"

"Nah. Not if you don't want to. There's nothing sacred about conventional framing."

"Hey, I don't know what to want, okay? So I'd rather do it right."

She put her fists on both hips. "What does *right* mean? Some book's way? Some grown-up's way?"

"Fine. Great. So what I really feel like doing is turning it on and laying it down on the stupid carpet. How's that?"

"Then do it. It'll look like MTV."

Gabriel let the camera slip from his shoulder and hang at arm's length, looking at Tess out of the corner of his eye. She wore black high tops, black spandex bicycling pants, and a sweatshirt that featured a reindeer on a chaise. Underneath that were the words HAVE A KICK-BACK CHRISTMAS.

"We don't have a lot of money," Tess said, sounding edgy, "and this is one hundred percent cotton marked down from about fifty-five dollars to three."

"I didn't say anything."

"You didn't have to. Your face said it for you. Close-ups don't lie." Then she tapped her pointy nose. "And before you start registering any more anally fixated middle-class judgments, it's *my* nose. Mine. Just like my mother's before she had it done for *Embers Don't Last* and forever lost her chance to be cast in anything really interesting or to be anybody who wasn't just pretty."

"I wasn't looking at your nose, okay?"

"Well, you would've, because you're a scrutinizer. Do you know what *scrutiny* means?"

"Yeah. Do you know what *paranoid* means?"

They glared at each other for a few seconds—Tess with her mouth crooked as if somebody in a hurry had drawn it on, Gabriel with his jaw set.

"Tell you what," she said finally. "Just shoot me coming in the door; then we'll decide what to do next. Okay?"

"I guess."

"Good. So I'm gonna go out, wait a sec, come back in, talk, and that's it. Got it?"

"It's not exactly the formula for creating life in the laboratory. I got it."

When he was by himself, Gabriel wiped both hands on his jeans, swung the camcorder up, and found the trigger. "Okay!"

The door swung open. "July twenty-first," she said toward the built-in microphone. "I meet Gabriel, the new kid." Then she smiled—her teeth were as startlingly white as her mom's—and motioned. "Gimme."

"The camera? What for?"

She took it smoothly. "Just stand there."

"I don't have acne, either. And my bed isn't rumpled. I made it myself."

She waved her free hand as though she were wiping a blackboard clean. "No, no. This is different."

Gabriel thought he could feel the lens crawl slowly all over him, like a caterpillar. "What?" he asked finally.

"Nothing." And she ended with his face. "That's all. That's it. They go together. I say I met you; then there's a picture of you."

"For what?"

"Call it posterity." Then she cut the distance between them right in half with one step and said, "So, I'm going down to the studio to get more film for old Bessie here, right?" She patted her camera.

"Which studio, where my dad is?"

"Uh-uh. Another one. It's just, you know, over there— one bus ride, no transfers." He watched her tongue roam around inside her mouth.

"Look," she said finally. "If it doesn't matter, I think my mother would like it if you went. Which would make my life a little easier. But it's up to you."

Gabriel shrugged. "How much weirder could it get?"

Downstairs, Mona sat by the edge of the lap pool, paging through a magazine so thin it must have been for people who didn't like to read. Spotting him and Tess on the stairs, she stood up and waved.

Mona reminded Gabriel of someone he'd seen on reruns of TV shows, the ones in black and white. Not that she was anywhere near as old as black-and-white TV, but she wore tight turquoise pants that ended way above her bare ankles, a white blouse with the collar turned up, and a bracelet made out of seashells. If she'd had a tall drink with a little umbrella in it, and if some guy with big puffy sleeves had been playing the marimba in the background, she'd have fit right in. And Tess with her camera and him in his five-pocket fatigue pants would have been the ones out of place.

"Did you sleep?" she asked, smiling at him.

"Uh-huh."

"Need anything—toothpaste, juice, toilet paper?"

Toilet paper? Gabriel squirmed. "No, thanks."

Mona held out a small rose-colored bag with a white handle. The word BRIANA was written on both sides. "I made some sandwiches for later."

"Gee, Mrs. Miller. I just ate."

"It's Mona. And you'll get hungry later."

Gabriel heard the slap of water and glanced at the lap pool a half dozen yards away. Someone turned and headed the other way. His arm, almost exactly the same color as his trunks, arced through the air in slow motion.

Glancing back, the Briana bag was still hanging there, held by Mona's slender fingers.

"Uh," said Gabriel. "I, uh . . ."

"He doesn't want to carry it," said Tess. "Because it's pink, right?"

"No, I'm just not hungry."

"If it was black and from the Clint Eastwood Mayhem Center, you wouldn't mind, though, would you?"

"I don't mind. I'm just not . . ."

"Wait'll your dad finds out you spurned my mother's selfless generosity."

Mona told her daughter that Gabriel didn't have to take it if he didn't want to. "And," she assured him, "I'm not going to tell Sumner anything."

"All right. All right. I'll take it."

He'd just tucked the bag under his arm, at least hiding that stupid mini–rope handle, when there was a small commotion at the other end of the lap pool. The swimmer had slithered up two of the three wide steps and lay across the last one, breathing heavily. Then he crawled halfway into the still air. Then he stood up slowly, mouth open, gazing about bewildered. It was as if he were acting out the stages of evolution.

Gabriel took a step backward.

"It's just Mr. Palmer," said Tess.

"Yeah, but . . ."

Mona turned around, and they all watched Mr. Palmer make his way toward them. He looked slightly curved: a grade of C made by a hurried teacher. The skin on his chest and thighs hung like drapery, but there were muscles under there—ropy and taut. His hair was white, matted to his scalp and chest. And genitals.

"Close your mouth," Tess whispered, and Gabriel did as Mona's arm settled over the old man's bare shoulders.

"Mr. Palmer, this is Gabriel McKay. His father wrote *Timmy the Otter*. Remember I showed you that sweet little book? Well, Gabriel's dad is out here working for Oxley Studios. They have big plans for Timmy." Mona spoke slowly and enunciated every word.

Mr. Palmer focused on Gabriel. His eyes were the deepest blue Gabriel had ever seen, not sky blue or gem blue but sea blue, with depths below depths in them. One hand rose slowly from his bare thigh.

"Gabriel's a wonderful name," he said in a deep voice. "A wonderful choice."

Gabriel shook his hand gingerly. "My mom picked it."

His smile, like everything else about him, was deliberate. "Yes, but you, too. On another plane, of course."

Using her fingers, Mona started to comb Mr. Palmer's hair back into place. "We're going to have a dinner Friday night. Sumner's coming, and Gabriel, I hope. Cassandra, of course. Can you make it?"

He took a deep breath. "I believe so, yes."

"Fine. See you then. Say sevenish?"

His gaze, like a warm hand, touched each of them. Then he turned around and walked away.

Tess, standing beside Gabriel, remarked, "It's just a butt. Everybody's got one."

Mona said that Gabriel probably wasn't used to nudists.

"He's a nudist?"

"What'd you think?" Tess said. "World's oldest slow-motion exhibitionist?"

"How am I supposed to know? Jeez, up walks this naked old Hawaiian and I'm supposed to deduce he's—"

"Hawaiian!" Tess snorted. "You think Palmer is a Hawaiian name? Are you kidding? Palmanikaknackanoeni, maybe. But not just Palmer." Tess was laughing pretty hard.

"But his skin's so dark."

"He's a nudist, gumball. He's been out in the sun for about seventy years."

"He's seventy?"

"Ninety, actually," Mona interjected. "He discovered nudism when he was twenty. He met his wife at Sunny Acres, up near Santa Barbara. She passed away just a little more than a year ago." She turned to watch Mr. Palmer, who was almost to one of the ground-floor apart-

36

ments. "It hasn't been an easy time for him. They were married sixty-seven years."

Mona looked thoughtful for a second, then sighed and bent down gracefully to pick up her copy of *Daily Variety*.

"Toby called," she said, looking at Tess and sounding very brisk all of a sudden. "There might be some work next week, but I have to dress up like an aspirin. Do I want to do that?"

"Not if it's going to give you a headache," her daughter replied.

Mona laughed soundlessly, took a quick glance in Mr. Palmer's direction, and lifted a wadded-up Kleenex to her nose, which reminded Gabriel that it wasn't her real nose, or at least not the original. She'd had it worked on. It seemed to him nearly perfect. Maybe he could ask her sometime about his enormous hands and feet or his skinny neck. Maybe get a neckectomy while he was out here.

"See you guys later," Mona said. "Be careful." When she leaned to kiss her daughter, Tess ducked and began to inspect the mechanism of her camera. Then she took off across the relentlessly green artificial turf.

"Moms are a pain," she said as Gabriel caught up with her.

"Tell me about it. Mine about puts my eye out with her stupid racing helmet every time she tries to hug me, but she's nothing compared to my dad."

Just inside the foyer, an odd little nonplace with a miniature chandelier and a lopsided table, they ran into a mail carrier in blue knee-length shorts and one of those pith helmets people used to wear in movies about Africa.

"Hey, Tess," he said, holding out a package. "I was just going to take Mr. Palmer his vitamins."

"Leave 'em if you want. I'll drop it off when we come back." Then she pointed to Gabriel. "Better start looking for McKay—Gabriel or Sumner." Then she nudged Gabriel. "This is Bob."

"You in the business?" Bob asked as he shook hands.

Gabriel glanced at Tess. "Uh, I don't think so."

"Sumner is. He's a writer, but I'll bet he hasn't got final cut."

Bob shook his head woefully. "Mona," he explained, "got me in the Extras Guild. I'm very big in crowd scenes." Then he grinned and tossed a few bills onto the table. "Where's Cassandra?" he asked, reaching for the door. "You'd think she'd know these were coming?"

Outside, Tess watched Bob disappear before she raised her camera. "Let me get a shot of you in those shades."

But Gabriel put one hand out, covering the lens like a shy movie star or a crooked stockbroker.

"Wait a minute. First, let's get something straight. It's not gumball; it's Gabriel."

"Who said anything about gumballs?"

"You did." He pointed. "You called me gumball back there when we were talking about Mr. Palmer."

"Oh, that. Well, you sounded like a gumball."

"We don't have a lot of nudists in Bradleyville, okay? We tend to keep our pants on when we meet somebody for the first time."

"Gee, and my geography teacher said Missouri was the Show Me State."

"Very funny. But no more weird names, okay?"

Tess had attached a long colorful strap to the camcorder, so she raised both hands to show her compliance. "Fine. Now can I get you in a shot, Mr. Lord of the Gumballs, or are you gonna pout?"

"What'd I say a minute ago!"

"To not call you a gumball. And I didn't. I called you Lord of the Gumballs, which is different."

Gabriel kept his teeth clenched. "No gumballs of any kind."

"Aw, I'm just pulling your chain. Relax." She took him by one arm, and they walked toward the oleander bushes that grew in front of the salmon-colored building. "Right here," she said.

As Tess peered through the viewfinder, backed up, and waved Gabriel a little this way and a little that, he glanced over one shoulder. Above him in huge letters hung the building's number—1115—and its name—The Harmony Arms. Not in block letters like the names on the stores in Bradleyville, but in flowing script as if it had been written by a passing goddess.

Tess frowned. "I'm trying to get *Arms* out of the way," she said, squatting down. "All I want to see is your face with those sunglasses and above it the word *Harmony*. The script calls for a little irony."

"What script?"

She tapped her forehead as she went to one knee and took three or four seconds' worth of film. Then she said, "Let's go, Elvis."

"And who's this Elvis?"

"Elvis Miyata. He's the star of *The Big Nap*."

Gabriel looked puzzled.

"You've never seen *The Big Sleep?* Humphrey Bogart and Lauren Bacall? God, are you deprived."

"I've *taken* a nap. Does that count?"

Tess laughed out loud. "I like it that you're surly. Elvis needs to have an edge."

They sat on the bench and waited for the bus. Miles away, to the east, Gabriel could see mountains. They looked packed for storage, wrapped in dirty cloths.

"Is that smog?" he asked finally.

"Uh-huh. And if we were up there looking down here, we'd be buried in it, too."

"Where I live, that's all you hear about California: smog, earthquakes, and people shooting each other."

"We try to keep busy."

"Have you ever been in an earthquake?"

"Sure."

"Were you scared?"

"I guess." She ran one hand affectionately over her camera. "They're always over before I can get old Bessie cranked up. Mostly things just shake and then guys come on TV selling bottled water."

Gabriel watched the cars for a little while. Lots of them were big and shiny. Inside, people were talking on car phones.

"No, they're not talking to each other," Tess said.

Gabriel grinned for just about the first time that day. "I was just thinking that."

"Is it as different for you out here," Tess asked, "as I think it is?"

"There's like three traffic signals in Bradleyville."

"I'd die."

"Maybe not. From any of the decks at Mom's, you can see trees and pastures and then a ridge and beyond that more trees."

"Nice view if you're a wolverine, maybe."

Just then a bus pulled up, but before Gabriel could get to his feet, Tess shook her head. "Not ours."

He read the advertisement on the side. Even though it was in Spanish, he guessed the word *accidente* right above the photo of a lawyer trying hard to look concerned. Over that, though, were swirls of spray paint—a lot of peculiar-looking names and numbers that were more foreign-looking than anything from just across a simple border. They could have been from way back in time, too: Mayan, maybe. Or Aztec. It made him feel very pale and thin.

Tess ducked her head as exhaust engulfed them for a couple of seconds. "Did you know the singular for *graffiti* is *graffito*?" she asked.

"I've never seen one graffito, have you?"

"Nah. They're like peanuts. There's no such thing as just one."

"I'm used to seeing BEAT THE KAHOKS or BOB LOVES SUE. But just on big boulders or in the bathrooms at school."

She looked in the direction the bus had taken. "There's some of that, but mostly it's gang stuff. Kind of like cats spraying—'I own this.' 'This is mine.' 'I was here first.'"

"And the people who do it fight over territory and stuff?"

"Yeah. Over drugs mainly. But not like in *West Side*

Story, with Natalie Wood and Richard Beymer. Nobody's singing, 'I'm too woozy to aim my Uzi.' They just pop each other."

Gabriel looked around. "Each other, right? Not regular people like us."

"Not on purpose, usually. Not unless you're in the way."

Tess got up, trotted a few yards into the street, and peered west. Then she sat down again.

"Busbusbusbusbusbus," she said in an intense half-whisper. Before Gabriel could ask, she explained: "Makes it get here faster."

"Oh, sure."

Just then the big white number 441 with the red and orange stripes turned the corner a couple of blocks away and cruised toward them.

"Amazing!"

"When we get on," Tess instructed, "don't look at people, okay?"

Gabriel stopped searching in his pockets for change. "Huh?"

"I said don't stare at anybody." She sounded serious.

"Okay, but I wouldn't. . . ."

Then she reached across him. "And I'll carry this pink, obviously effeminate bag, the one that casts serious doubt on your masculinity and will cause a wave of derision to sweep through the bus the minute you step aboard."

"Very funny." Gabriel eased up to the curb beside her.

Tess climbed the two big steps, deposited her money, and snatched a narrow transfer. "For the way back," she explained.

Gabriel followed, fumbling with the bulky camcorder, trying unsuccessfully to get his free hand deep enough into one front pocket.

"How much?" he asked.

The driver never took his eyes off the street, never moved, never blinked. "Dollar ten."

Gabriel held out a bill.

"Exact change," intoned Robo-Driver.

"But I don't—"

Tess dropped the money in for him and plucked a transfer free.

"He's from Missouri," she said, grinning. Then she led the way to an empty seat.

"Will you not say, 'He's from Missouri,' like all we do back there is sit around with our hound dogs and watch the three traffic lights change?"

"Hey, I was surprised when you pulled out that twenty. I thought you might have a big chunk of salt or a pelt."

Gabriel made a face.

She raised her camera. "Hold that sneer." She began to narrate: "Elvis didn't need a .44 in a shoulder holster. His sarcasm could tear through a mobster like hot lead." Then she flattened herself against the seat to let him in. "C'mon, sit by the window."

"Is it okay if I look at the palm trees, or are there rules against that, too?"

Gabriel slid past, laid the camera on his lap, crossed both hands over it, and peered out. They were riding parallel to an enormous cement trench. In the center, little bushes grew in pools of standing water.

"L.A. River," Tess said without being asked.

"Yeah, there's Huck and Jim now on that designer raft."

Tess laughed and whispered into the microphone on her recorder as Gabriel read the graffiti on the sloping banks, letters sometimes ten feet high in red and black, yellow and purple, green and white—all the colors he was used to seeing on the wings and bellies of birds.

"What's *CHAKA?*" he asked after seeing it for the tenth time.

"Just some egomaniac tagger. He's everywhere."

Gabriel read the rest under his breath, wondering how to pronounce Vato or El Gran Jacinto.

"Most of the other stuff," Tess explained, "is just somebody's name, gang signs, maybe messages or something."

"While back in Bradleyville, we still call each other on the phone."

When the bus swung off the freeway, Gabriel read the names of the stores. He was kind of relieved to see ones he recognized like the Gap, Sears, and an inevitable McDonald's.

"Pretty much what you expected?" Tess asked a few minutes later.

"I guess. Maybe I thought everything would be a little more California."

"Meaning?"

"Oh, I don't know. Just . . . I know better, okay? But in a way it's like home: cars, stores, clocks. I guess I thought somehow that people in California didn't have to work or shop or anything. They were just *in* California."

"Doing what? Naming the animals and washing their hair in little waterfalls?"

"I know, I know: It sounds stupid." He turned sideways. "How long did it take you to get used to L.A.?"

"I was born here."

Gabriel rubbed his stomach. "I think it makes me nervous."

"Yeah, that's what I like about it." Then she raised her camera and sighted straight up at the ceiling.

Gabriel began to count the people on the street who were carrying what looked like narrow lunch pails. But smaller. Snack pails?

"Car radios," Tess informed him. "So they won't get stolen."

"I know what a car radio is," Gabriel said. "What I can't figure out is how you know what I'm thinking."

She rubbed at her right eye. "I just pretend it's all new to me, too. You can't be a filmmaker with tired eyes. It's got to be fresh every day." She leaned in, and Gabriel smelled the soap she used. "It's good for me that you're out here. You remind me to wake up. Otherwise, *The Big Nap* will turn out to be *The Big Snooze.*"

"You're really making a movie?"

"Sure. Kind of a mystery-comedy. Maybe an *After-School Special*, maybe a feature. I don't know yet. That's not important. What's important is to get some footage every day. Just do that and the film will tell you what it wants to be. All I know is it's for kids, because I got no real use for grown-ups."

"What's wrong with grown-ups?"

"For one thing, they're just too gross: the men get erections and the women have babies."

Gabriel slipped down in his seat. He was positive that someone, probably the driver, would stomp down the aisle and throw them off the bus.

"Oh, yeah," Tess added. "And they're way too hairy."

"Your mother's not hairy," he whispered.

"Oh, grow up. She goes down to Randi's about every twenty minutes and has her entire body waxed."

"Waxed?"

"Yeah. What do women do in Bradleyville, scrape their legs with a clam shell? Out here they pay to get like dipped in hot wax, and then somebody rips that off and the hair goes with it."

"You're kidding."

"Uh-uh." She shook her head so hard the rest of her body quivered. "But worst of all is they've lost their childlike quality, you know? Which is the one thing a great artist has to have. I mean look at Salvador Dalí or Woody Allen. They got older, but they're not grown-ups." She stood up then and squinted. "Almost there. The stop after next."

Gabriel sat up slowly, like a wary seal surfacing.

Outside, catty-corner from their bus, a dozen or so men—mostly young, all with hair black and shiny as new catechisms—stood or leaned or sat. As Gabriel watched, a white van with ladders roped to its top pulled up.

Immediately the crowd on the corner rose as one thing and surrounded the paint-splattered Chevrolet. It reminded Gabriel of the way birds explode from one spot in a cornfield, then settle again. Some of the men clamored at the two side windows; the rest waved frantically and leapt in the air.

Then the door on the passenger side opened, three or four men disappeared inside, and the van pulled away. Two dozen pairs of eyes gazed after it enviously. Two dozen hands dove into as many shallow pockets.

"What was that all about?" Gabriel asked.

"Work," Tess explained without looking back. "All those guys are up from Mexico or South America. This is *el norte,* which means the north, which means job heaven. If five bucks an hour every now and then is your idea of heaven."

"My dad talked about California like it was heaven sometimes."

"Yeah, but he's got a job. Those guys don't, *and* since they don't have green cards, they have to watch out for immigration, too." She half-stood to check a street sign. "About two months ago, *la migra* picked up about fifteen of them right by the Harmony Arms."

"For doing what?" Gabriel asked.

"Nothing. Looking for work. So while they're waiting for the bus that'll take 'em back to Mexico, Mom comes out with sandwiches and Kool-Aid and Cassandra tells their fortunes." She fiddled with her camera. "File that under Conflicting Views of the United States, right?"

Just then the bus stopped with a lurch, the front door opened, and a thin man got on, breathing hard, and made his way down the aisle.

He had longish godforsaken hair and a stringy dog's beard, and his long green coat with its torn places hanging loose and flapping made Gabriel think of snakes he'd seen shedding their skin. And the way the people on either side of him leaned away was what the tall grasses did when a cottonmouth made its way toward some damp, shady place.

With a thump, he sat down across the aisle. Not facing forward but facing them. Looking them over.

Tess stared straight ahead, so Gabriel tried, but he couldn't help glancing out of the corner of his eye.

47

"Lemme zee add gamera," the man blurted out.

Gabriel's heart started to thud. When he swallowed, everything stopped right in the center of his chest. Tess's left hand slid over his. "Act like you're going to hand it over," she whispered, "but start shooting instead."

"What?"

"You don't want that," Tess said, turning away from Gabriel. Then she unzipped the fanny pack slung around her waist. "This is better."

The man leaned forward, blinking, as Tess unfolded a dollar.

"Wha zat?" he mumbled, still trying to focus.

"Start the camera!" she hissed at Gabriel without looking at him.

But Gabriel could only stare, open-mouthed.

"It's twenty dollars." She snapped the bill enticingly. "That's a lot better than having to sell the camera. Take it. It's real money."

Just as the drunk groped for the bill, the bus lurched to a stop, sending him off the curved plastic seat and into a heap on the floor.

Tess fumbled for Gabriel's hand. "This," she said, "is where we get off." And she jumped over the man's writhing body. "C'mon," she urged.

Gabriel swallowed hard. "He'll grab me!"

"He won't grab you. C'mon. Jump."

The man made it to his knees, reached for the nearest chrome bar, missed, and collapsed again.

Tess hurdled him again and shoved Gabriel toward the front door.

He was glad that Tess was hustling him away from the

bus stop because it gave his feet a chance to catch up with his heart, which was racing. Every dozen yards or so, he glanced over one shoulder, afraid the bus would screech to a halt and that creep would come howling down the street after them.

When Tess slowed down and glanced at her watch, Gabriel felt his damp forehead. "Was that my fault? I mean I only looked at the guy for a second."

"A second is all it takes, but if it makes you feel any better, that one would've hassled us, anyway."

"Jeez, I've been here about thirty-six hours, and I've seen a skating psychic, an ancient nudist, and I've watched you jump back and forth over a psychopath. You could live in Bradleyville your whole life and never see even one of those things."

Tess shrugged it off. "That guy was just drunk. I mean you see people like that a few times, pretty soon you learn how to read 'em, right?"

Gabriel tried a grin. "If we want to read back home, we go to the library." He looked back one more time. "I was scared stiff."

"Really?" She slowed down some more. "It's cool that you can say that. A lot of guys would be like, 'Lucky you got to him first. I was just about to tear his head off and bowl with it.'" She raised her camera. "Elvis Miyata gets vulnerable."

Gabriel turned his face away. "C'mon, cut it out."

Tess made a half-circle. "Your profile is good," she said, still filming away. "Really good from the left." Then she stopped and handed him the camera. "Take me now."

"What for?"

"Never mind. Just do it."

Gabriel hefted the big Panasonic. "You're in *The Big Nap*, too?"

"Uh-uh. This is for *Mondo Tess*."

"What's that?"

She smiled one of those big I-just-won-first-prize-in-the-spelling-bee smiles. "The story of my life from the age of twelve on. Like a self-documentary. Do you know what *mondo* means?"

"I bet I will in a minute."

"World. *The World of Tess*. I borrowed it from *Mondo Cane*, this campy old exploitation film. I started like sixteen months ago when Mom got me the camcorder, and I film every important thing that happens to me. That's why I wanted you to get that action on the bus."

"Oh, sorry."

"That's okay. It'll probably happen again."

Gabriel gulped and made a face. "I can hardly wait."

"Anyhow," Tess said, "I'm gonna go to film school when I'm eighteen, twenty max; I take my senior project with me, and all I have to do is edit it."

"*Mondo Tess?*"

She nodded vigorously. "Almost a decade of raw stock turns into a heart-stopping psychological thriller, a film of sweeping emotional power, a stunner, a rare and precious film, dense with detail, packed with wit."

Gabriel picked up the rhythm: "Two thumbs up. Four stars. On a scale of one to ten: an eleven."

"Exactly. Good for you."

"We do get movie reviews in Bradleyville. They're just a little late because they have to be packed in by mules."

About a block later, they came to a wide driveway,

turned up it, and stopped outside a glassed-in booth that opened on both sides. While Tess peeked in and started talking to one of the uniformed guards, Gabriel looked at the huge advertisements that flanked the drive. They were basically billboards brought down to eye level, so the people on them looked like monsters—lips big as canoes, each tooth thick and white as an ice chest.

"C'mon," Tess said, sticking a day pass onto his blue polo shirt.

Gabriel followed her past square bungalows with enormous letters on their sides.

Then he asked, "So is this like where my dad works?"

"Uh-uh. He's at a *film* studio. This is mostly schlock TV. Ever seen *Billy's Bait Shop?*"

Gabriel shook his head. "Mom lets me watch about a minute of TV a year, so I save up for baseball season."

"It's just three old farts in bib overalls sitting around telling lies until these girls come in to buy worms and almost fall out of their halter tops. Mom was on it once." Tess glanced at her watch. "Toby won't be back from lunch for maybe ten minutes." She held up the pink Briana bag. "Want to eat?"

They hunkered down on the warm asphalt in the shade of Producers' Building D. Tess shook the bag, then upended it as if she were playing some weird game of chance. Out tumbled two sandwiches wrapped in flowered paper towels and two bags of corn chips.

"They're both the same," she assured him. "Tofu egg salad."

"What's that?"

"It's better if you don't know. Just eat."

They chewed in silence for a little while. When a

guard on a tiny motorbike putted by, Gabriel asked Tess, "No one's going to care if we sit here, are they?"

She looked over at him, squinting. "Who's gonna care, the shade police? This is L.A., kid. Anything goes here. Even something as radical as eating lunch."

"God, forget I asked."

She swung her unopened bag of chips lightly and hit his thigh with it. "I'm just runnin' lines past myself. Who knows when I'll say something cool, like 'the shade police.' Maybe I can use that in a script sometime. So don't take me seriously. All right?" She tapped him again. "Gabriel?"

"All right, I guess."

"So tell me about your dad. Is it true what Mom said, that he's making an animal movie?"

"Not really." Gabriel frowned and lifted the top piece of bread: it *looked* like egg salad, anyway. "Did you read *Timmy the Otter?*"

"Yeah. Mom showed me—cute little otter, drama around the pond, happy ending. Not *Godfather IV*, but okay. Your dad did the whole thing, right? Wrote it, drew it, the works."

"Uh-huh. Then remember about six months ago, when that oil tanker, *Queen of the Seas*, ran aground?"

"Sort of."

"Well, there was this picture on some network news show of a real otter all covered with oil, and this blond anchorwoman shakes her head and just sort of spontaneously says, 'Now my daughter is going to cry herself to sleep tonight. She thinks all those little guys are Timmy.' The next thing you know studios are calling Dad and bidding for rights to the book."

"Wow. It's all timing, isn't it? And Sumner's, what? Creative consultant for the project, I guess?"

"Uh-huh."

"Did he get the final cut?"

"Huh?"

"The final say-so on what goes and what stays in the movie."

Gabriel shrugged. "I don't think so. He never said anything. . . ."

Tess sagged. "Those studio jerks will probably turn it into *Tommy the Oyster*. If he's lucky."

"Dad said they were really nice on the phone and they kept talking about the integrity of the work and stuff like that."

Tess rolled her gray eyes. "Between you and me, what people say on the phone out here doesn't always count. The phone's like"—she pointed straight up—"skywriting, you know? Big words that blow away." She glanced at her watch, where the black hands lay almost side by side on the turquoise face. "You ready?"

Gabriel got up in sections, as usual: planting his big feet, putting his big hands on his knees, unfolding. Then he brushed at his pants, first the back, then the front.

"Are we neat and clean enough now?" Tess asked. "Or should I ring for the butler?"

Gabriel flushed. "This is just you talking to yourself, right, making up dialogue or something? And it only *sounds* like you're giving me a hard time."

"Now you got it."

They set off across the corner of a parking lot with names capping each rectangular space. Gabriel could see how new some of them were and how a layer of fresh white paint covered an old name so the new one could be stenciled in black.

"Makes you feel real secure," commented Tess.

"I wonder if Dad's got one of those."

"Probably the paint's not even dry yet."

Minivans cruised by, hauling lumber. Three young guys in jeans passed, each of them carrying a stuffed fish. Gabriel was gawking when he tripped, then caught himself just as Tess grabbed for the back of his shirt.

Flustered, he explained, "I was, uh, thinking."

She took his arm as if he were older than Mr. Palmer. "Promise me you won't think and drive."

He laughed in spite of himself, tried to hold a door for her, then let himself be pushed inside.

Tess said, "You were asking yourself, 'Where are the movie stars?' right?"

He was starting to get used to the way she read his mind. "Yeah, a little. Or a horse and chariot. Or a volcano, maybe." *Or showgirls in a plume or two and not much else.*

"Working in television's just like working in a factory—a laugh every thirty seconds, a commercial every eight minutes. That's why I'm going to *film* school. I'd kill myself if *The Big Nap* kept getting interrupted by a bunch of guys drinking beer in the woods."

"I thought you said it might be for an *After-School Special.* That's television."

Tess stopped abruptly. "You remembered I said that?"

"Sure."

"That was like a slip, but I thought, 'Ah, he's not really listening, anyway.' But you were. Amazing."

He followed her down a hall then, past open doors where secretaries worked on computers and worried-looking guys waited by the printer.

Tess skidded to a stop and held out one arm like a school crossing guard. "Wait," she whispered. "You know Lex Bollocks, the guy who hosts *Dive for Your Dictionary?*"

"Maybe."

She pointed. "Well, that's him."

Gabriel watched a short man in a double-breasted suit drink from a paper cup, then stare at himself in the upside-down water bottle.

Gabriel whispered, "He's about three feet tall."

"Doesn't matter." She motioned for him. "Come here."

Tess led the way through two double doors and into a dim studio. The *Dive for Your Dictionary* logo was scrawled across a phony collection of books. Tess went and stood beside Lex's podium. Then she stepped behind it and was immediately a foot taller.

"So," she explained, "nobody's ever bigger than the star of the show." She pointed. "Look behind where the contestants stand."

Gabriel leaned to see an upholstered trench. When he stepped in, he could hardly see over the glass plate where the answers were scrawled.

When they met in the center of the set he said, "And it's like miniature. On TV it looks huge."

Tess held up two fingers. "One, don't believe anything you hear on the phone, and two, don't believe anything you see on a TV screen."

"Even the egg salad isn't egg salad out here."

Tess gave him a decisive thumbs-up, then led him down another hall, past a door with a blinking red light and right into an office where a young woman wearing an I Survived Catholic School T-shirt smiled at Tess and nodded an okay.

As Gabriel passed her, she asked, "Protestant, right?"

"Yes, ma'am."

"It figures."

The man behind the glass-topped desk might have been drawn by a first-grader: his bald head was perfectly round. And that was balanced on a round body.

"Tess!" he boomed, pushing himself up and plodding out to shake her hand.

"Toby, this is my friend Gabriel."

Toby hitched up his white pants and looked at Gabriel critically.

"Interesting profile. Better from the left."

Tess grinned.

"I see you sort of floundering down the court in some inferior brand of athletic shoe, those size twelves of yours going every which way. Then we cut to you in the sponsor's brand and you're making lay-ups like Michael Jordan. Right, Tess?"

"Right, Toby."

"He's too thin for pancake mix and too young for toilet paper. He's shoes. Right, Tess?"

"Right, Toby."

"Leave your name and phone number with Our Lady of Perpetual Complaints out there." Then he reached for a box. "Here's your film. Do good work now, you hear? And tell your mom to call me if she wants the dancing aspirin. Otherwise I need an all-weather tire with long legs, but she's gotta get wet. Right, Tess?"

"Right, Toby."

He frowned at Gabriel once more. "Maybe in a few years, something with caffeine, 'cause you've got the right hair for caffeine. But for now, what can I tell you—you're shoes."

Once they were back in the hall, Gabriel offered to help Tess with the cardboard box.

"I can get it," she said. "You handle the camera."

"Toby makes commercials, I guess."

"He couldn't resist the big bucks, but if I had to watch any commercials, I'd watch his. He's pretty good."

"And he just gives you this stuff?"

Tess lodged the carton against the wall, wiped both hands on her slick black pants, and got a better grip.

"Sort of. He doesn't like to use these cassettes too many times, so after a while he just slips 'em to me, and I film over the little screen tests or the dancing pork chops or whatever."

"I guess I wondered how you could afford to film your whole life."

"Yeah. No Toby, no *Mondo Tess*."

"And he's a friend of the family?"

"Exactly. From way back. Before VCRs even."

Then they just stood there. Finally Tess turned and looked at him.

"What?" said Gabriel finally.

"You lead."

"Me? Why me?"

"'Cause I'm not always gonna be with you. So, c'mon.

Get us out of here and back to the corner; then pick the right bus." She nudged him with the box.

Gabriel slapped at the sharp corner. "What is this, basic training?"

Tess grinned at him over the tucked-in flaps. "It's a jungle out there, kid."

About a week later, Gabriel was getting dressed in a hurry because he and Sumner were due at Mona's for dinner at seven.

He picked one of his five shirts and stared. It was the color of Nyquil cough syrup. *Way too bright*, Gabriel thought. Nothing like the ones he saw on other kids in the Westside Pavilion.

He threw it down, turned to the full-length mirror, and looked at his narrow chest, where almost every rib showed. Once in fifth grade he'd seen a movie on archeology. College kids in khaki shorts crouched around a skeleton stuck in a hillside and worked away at its ribs with soft brushes. That's what Gabriel thought he looked like sometimes—a walking fossil.

Finally he grabbed the white one and struggled into it, arms waving, head thrown back as if he'd been underwater too long. Then he wandered down the hall toward his father's room. He heard him before he saw him, heard the rustle of waxed paper and knew that Sumner was pigging out, and Gabriel knew why.

"They're not still trying to get you to buy into *Robo-Otter*, are they?" he asked, leaning on the closed door.

"Not exactly." His mouth was full, though, so it came out muffled.

"Or *Teenage Mutant Ninja Otter?*"

"Probably not. And just about the time I think we're never even going to get off the storyboard, Miles says he's got people in preproduction. But I'm not so sure. Mona says they're capable of anything."

Gabriel heard his dad pick up the animal crackers, heard the crackle, imagined the colorful little boxes, each one yellow and red with painted tigers behind the painted bars.

"You can come in if you want to, Gabriel. I'm almost ready."

"I'm okay." He didn't like to see his father undressed. That big sloping body depressed him.

"Tell me what you and Tess did today."

"Went to Melrose Avenue."

Gabriel heard a dresser drawer slide. "Was it fun?"

"I guess. We saw some rock 'n' roll guy carrying a boa constrictor around his neck. Otherwise it was just people with cameras gawking at each other."

"Isn't Melrose a long way from here?"

Gabriel heard his father cross the room, heard the slap of after-shave, heard the click the Old Spice bottle made when he put it down.

"Gabriel? Isn't Melrose a long way?"

"Yeah, Dad. Sort of. But Tess could get to the moon on a bus. She really knows her way around."

Sumner stepped into the hall, fiddling with the waistband of his light blue slacks. They were the kind that adjusted themselves, so somebody could gain or lose weight and not have to always buy new clothes.

"Dad, we don't need a couple of guys to do any work around here, do we?"

"Gosh, Gabriel, I don't think so." He looked around, frowning. "It relaxes me to clean, and besides that there's not much that needs doing."

"Tess and I keep seeing these guys up from Mexico and stuff." He turned to his father. "I know there are people who need work, but I never saw so many at one time." Gabriel smoothed his shirt, tucking it in tighter. "It makes me feel funny to be riding around with Tess without a care in the world."

"Big cities are all like that, I think. The difference between the haves and the have-nots is right out there."

"Boy, no kidding."

Sumner studied his son for a long time. "Want one?" he asked, holding out the last box of animal crackers. When Gabriel shook his head, Sumner offered the box to Timmy, who was slung over one shoulder, his brown wedge-shaped head resting on Sumner's soft chest.

"I can't tell you how glad I am it worked out that you and Tess can be friends. It's such a load off my mind."

Gabriel shrugged. "Tess is okay."

Sumner chose an elephant-shaped cracker, looked at it, frowned, and took something smaller—a seal. "We shouldn't forget, though, that she's not your buddy, okay? She's a girl."

"No problem. She's not my type, if I had a type. And I'm not her type, either. She doesn't like guys in general."

They'd reached the kitchen, and Sumner took a diet Hires out of the fridge, offered it to Gabriel, who shook his head, then opened it with a hiss.

"How do you know she doesn't like guys in general?" his dad asked before he took a drink.

"Well, we were waiting for the 43 bus outside this ice cream store, okay? This couple in a convertible drives up; the girl hops out and runs inside. While he's waiting, the guy checks out every girl on the street, including Tess."

Sumner pressed on his stomach, then belched. "And?"

"And she sort of snarled, 'That's men for you. They're all the same.'"

Sumner laughed. "She's an interesting young woman."

"Yeah, well, I'm just trying to tell you not to worry. We're not likely to run off to Las Vegas and get married."

Sumner smoothed Timmy's head, then slipped his arm into the flat, brown sleeve.

"Still," he said, brushing Timmy's white whiskers briskly, "you and I never really had one of those chats that fathers and sons usually have."

"I know that stuff from Health Ed. And Mom bought me a book, remember?"

Timmy swiveled his head around, "Sure," he piped, "but there are things that probably aren't in some old book, things that—"

Timmy's whiskers flew up as Gabriel grabbed his father's wrist with both hands. "I don't want to learn the facts of life from an otter, okay?" His voice soared, then cracked. "Any other father would . . . I mean most kids, when they talk to their dads about this . . . Aw, forget it. Let's just go eat."

▼ ▼ ▼

A few minutes later, standing in front of Mona's apartment, Sumner took a deep breath and tugged at his slacks.

"It's funny, isn't it," said Sumner, "to go to somebody's house that you don't know? Not like in Bradleyville."

Gabriel just nodded.

"Look," Sumner assured him, "you and I will have that, you know, conversation about, uh, you know what, later. Just the two of us, okay? Man to man."

"Sure, Dad."

Then he watched in disbelief as Timmy tapped on the blue door, right above the brass numbers. Then they waited. Timmy tried again, then covered his nose with both paws as the door swung open and Tess stood there.

She stepped aside. "Go on in, Sumner. Gabriel and I have to go down and get Mr. Palmer."

When the door closed behind his dad, Gabriel just stood there, staring out over the huge crater, the mounds of dirt, and the two-by-fours lying like an enormous game of Pick Up Sticks.

"If there was a pool down there," he muttered, "I think I'd jump. I might jump, anyway."

"If you do, can I have your room? It's bigger than mine."

Gabriel didn't even bother to glare at her. "I can't believe my dad sometimes," he said, starting slowly down the concrete steps.

"What happened?"

Gabriel stopped and turned to face her. "Do you think my dad's weird?" he asked earnestly.

Tess chomped at her gum. "Compared to who?"

"I just mean in general, I guess."

Her right hand came down firmly on his left shoulder. "There isn't any 'in general,' my friend. You can't take a picture of 'in general.' You can't put it in a movie."

Gabriel rubbed at his nose. "Compared to me, then. Is he weird compared to me?"

"You're different. You're a lot younger, and you're not a performer."

Gabriel looked incredulous. "Dad's not a performer."

"Get real. He's on all the time. He carries that puppet like I carry this camera."

"But you're not a performer."

"No, but I'm always ready. And so is your dad."

"But ready for what?"

Tess shrugged. "A line, a joke, an idea. Like I need to have old Bessie with me in case I see something I'm never gonna see again."

Gabriel thought this over. "But carrying a camera is a lot different from carrying a puppet."

"Look, I used to feel just like you do, about my folks I mean. Then Mr. Palmer told me to just let it go."

Gabriel frowned. "Let it go? What's that supposed to mean?"

"Not worry about it. Not obsess. Just, you know—let it go"—she let one arm drift upward—"like letting these balloons go that are full of resentment and anger and whatever."

"And it worked, just like that."

Tess brushed at some invisible dust on her camcorder's lens, then blew. "It can." Then she heard a noise—the low bumpety-bump of a table being moved, so she nudged Gabriel. "C'mon, we're gonna eat pretty soon."

They clattered downstairs together and made their way past the lap pool, dark now and as tranquil as one of the ponds around Bradleyville, then among the lounges and chairs until they got to Mr. Palmer's apartment, where the door stood partly open.

Gabriel put one hand on Tess's bare arm. "Hold it. He's not gonna be naked, is he?"

"Probably not. Want me to go first?"

"No, I can take it. I just want to be prepared."

Tess knocked softly, then peeked around the yellow door. "Mr. Palmer?" She slipped inside; then Gabriel heard her say, "It's okay. He's just asleep. Come on in."

As she leaned over Mr. Palmer and began to shake him very gently, Gabriel looked around. There were bright yellow curtains and a sunburst clock. Beside the tiny Formica bar that separated the kitchen from the living room stood a huge ceramic orange. On the pale walls hung framed pictures that Gabriel recognized from science class—the dark, explosive, and tumultuous face of the sun. There was some weird tingly music coming from somewhere.

"I must have dozed off," Mr. Palmer said, and Gabriel raised one hand in a modified wave.

"Take your time," Tess assured him. "Nobody's in a hurry."

Mr. Palmer stood up slowly, pushing away a crocheted blanket with a sunflower on it. Then he tugged at his loose cotton pullover and ran one hand slowly through his white hair.

"I'll just get my pumpkin seeds," he said, gesturing toward the kitchen. "Gabriel, you haven't been here before, have you? Look around. Make yourself at home."

"Let me show you something," Tess said, motioning for Gabriel to follow her down the hall, where she opened a door. As Gabriel leaned past her, she said, "Up there. It's the night sky, the way it used to be before, you know, smog and cars and stuff."

Gabriel looked at the violet ceiling with its pinpoints of white. "He painted this?"

"He and his wife." She gestured again. "That was their bed. I mean, it still is, you know, his."

Neatly made, it was covered by a huge black comforter graced with an embroidered moon. Across its face hung a single silver cloud.

Tess tugged Gabriel inside, where she nudged the bed and it sloshed. "Water, naturally." Then she pointed down. "And green carpet everywhere so it's like the earth." Then he followed her back down the hall and into the living room.

"Then this is day, see? Night back there; day up here." She gestured again and pointed to a photograph. "Look at this, when they were like twenty-five or something."

Gabriel leaned in. The woman was slender and blond, wearing sandals, a watch, and nothing else. One of her arms was around her partner's narrow waist. They were both smiling.

Gabriel was a little ashamed of what he was thinking. "Is this his wife?" he asked quickly.

"Yeah. Her name was Sunny. She was really nice." Tess led him from one framed photograph to another. "Famous nudists," she explained with a grin. "This guy was a mathematician, I think. This lady played the piano—you know, classical stuff. These guys were all doctors."

"Naked doctors. Too weird."

"Yeah. They're always ordering you to take *your* clothes off."

"Maybe they took turns telling each other."

Mr. Palmer shuffled back from the kitchen. He had a small plastic bag and, in each hand, an orange.

"Here you are," he said.

Gabriel glanced at Tess, who nodded, meaning, *Take it*.

"I have some freshly squeezed juice . . . ," Mr. Palmer began.

"We should probably go," Tess said.

"Yes, of course. Then just let me make sure . . ." He glanced around the room as a fly buzzed past Gabriel, who swatted at it, then reached for a piece of the *L.A. Times* lying nearby.

Mr. Palmer smiled and laid his warm hand on Gabriel's arm. "No, no," he said quietly. "He'll follow us out."

"It's just a fly."

Mr. Palmer started for the door. "I know, but as flies go, he's quite handsome, and he may have plans for the weekend." A smile spread across his face as slowly as if it were a photograph developing in a darkroom.

Gabriel and Tess went first as Mr. Palmer explained, "I'll just turn the lights off, you see, and he'll come right out."

Sure enough. Gabriel saw the insect zip past them and angle away. Then he followed Tess and Mr. Palmer past the lap pool. Gabriel liked how Tess led Mr. Palmer past the chairs and everything without making it obvious she was being extra careful.

"Did you swim today?" she asked politely.

"Oh, yes. Every day." Then he stopped with one hand on the black metal railing of the steps. "But it takes me twice as long to swim half as far." He turned to include

Gabriel. "Wonderful as they are—the elements, I mean—they stay the same while I decline." His skin was so dark it was hard for Gabriel to see his face. The white shirt and pants seemed to hang in the shadows. "I remember how my wife and I used to swim." He brightened a little, like a bulb attached to a generator someone was cranking by hand. "Miles and miles together. And then we'd go back to the cabin and make love and drop off to sleep."

Gabriel squirmed and stared at his feet as the door opened above them and a widening dune of light drifted down.

"There you all are," said Mona. "I was beginning to wonder."

Upstairs, the round table located in some ambiguous area between the dining room and the tiny kitchen had been extended, so the tablecloth with the cactus design on it was barely big enough.

Mona gave the sleeves of her turquoise T-shirt another roll. "You guys take the folding chairs, okay? They'll collapse under anybody else."

Tess put three fingers to her forehead and looked solemn. "Out of the mists that comprise the future, a picture emerges: Cassandra on her butt and all five of us can't get her up again."

"Shhh," said Mona, trying not to laugh out loud. "Help with the salad, please."

Tess acted like she was about to sail Gabriel a plate, Frisbee style. Then she just handed it over. "You hold; I'll scoop."

He stared at the enormous wooden bowl shaped like a canoe. "What's in here?" he asked, impressed.

"Just the usual—romaine, red leaf, cilantro, purple cabbage, hearts of palm, avocado, whatever."

Gabriel licked his lips. "Except for those fish sticks that got shoved to the back of the fridge, this is the first green thing I've seen in a week."

As Mona pointed to chairs and helped Mr. Palmer, Cassandra came out of the bathroom and up the short hall. She wore her Dodgers cap, one of those radios built into a headset, and a red muumuu that brushed the floor. She looked like an enormous campfire.

"I want to sit by Gabriel!" she demanded. "And adjust his aura."

Gabriel looked at her warily as Tess said, "Be careful. The last person she did this to is still in a coma."

Cassandra cackled. "Don't pay any attention to her, sweetie," and she leaned around to give Gabriel a big, noisy kiss on the cheek.

Tess whispered, "Now you've got like a big goober or something. Probably came out of her nose and stuck to your . . ."

As Gabriel pawed at his face she said, "Just kidding."

Cassandra tossed back her loose sleeves, rubbed her hands together briskly, and began to pat the air around Gabriel.

"Too much violet," she muttered. "What have you been doing?"

"Riding buses."

"Besides that." Cassandra closed her eyes. "Ah, talking to your mother, right?"

"Wow, yeah. She called from Calgary yesterday. How'd you—"

"Now, there's a restless soul."

69

Then she finished up—squinting, shaping the air, beginning to perspire. Finally she plopped down, drained her glass of wine, and poured another.

"How exactly do psychics work?" Sumner asked.

"Oh, different ways. Some of us get impressions or impulses. A few have a kind of meter in their heads that registers high or low. Some see pictures or hear voices. I used to know a couple who just felt hot or cold. I dream mostly. And sometimes things just come to me. You'd call them visions or hallucinations." She turned to Gabriel, who was eating politely with one hand in his lap. "I dreamed about this angel-child last night." She closed both eyes and leaned back. The radio hung around her neck, making her look like some ancient and weary aviator. "He's in his twenties and just drop dead gorgeous." Both hands rose from the table and she measured with her palms like a fisherman. "Shoulders like this."

"Oh, sure." Gabriel took two or three quick bites.

"No waist at all and the hips of a poet."

Gabriel began to really shovel it in then.

"Easy with those little lips," Tess quipped, "or you'll get fat poet's hips."

Everyone laughed in a good-natured way as Cassandra slipped on her earphones. "Excuse me. Top of the seventh," she said. "We're up."

"I've got fat hips," said Sumner, "and I'm not even a poet."

"The year I gained a lot of weight," Mona confided, "my therapist said it was body armor." She shook her head ruefully at the memory. "I was completely on my own, and Tess was just a little girl. I was so afraid."

"Well, Gabriel's almost grown, and I'm still scared."

When the silence started to bear down on everyone, Mona said brightly, "That's when my nutritionist made me start using these." She held up the chopsticks she'd been fiddling with. "They're so clumsy they make you slow down whether you want to or not."

Timmy rose from Sumner's lap and peeked over the edge of the table.

"Better keep those away from my friend Billy Beaver. He'll eat 'em for lunch."

Gabriel cringed, but Mona smiled and said firmly, "As far as being scared goes, I wouldn't be too hard on yourself, Sumner. It took courage to leave the things you knew and come out here." She made sure to include Gabriel as she raised her wineglass. "To the pioneers."

Mr. Palmer took a sip, then turned in his chair. He patted Timmy on the head. "If it's exercise you need, Sumner, and not body work by a professional, you could swim with me. There's very little that sun and air and water can't fix."

"Lord, I haven't swum in years and then not very well." Sumner picked up the chopsticks and had Timmy help him get the right grip. "But then I didn't come out here to be the same person I was back home, did I?"

Just then Cassandra slipped her earphones off, grinned, and reached for her wineglass, which was actually decorated with cowboy boots and made for iced tea.

"Seven to zip," she announced. "We're killin' 'em. This new shortstop up from Albuquerque just hit his second home run." Then she shook her head, poured more wine, and sighed.

"What?" Mona asked.

"Oh, just that I know Gabriel's going to have to struggle with his beauty and talent, too."

Gabriel snorted. "Oh, sure. Like right now I'm so talented at following Tess around that I'm thinking of branching out and following other people, too."

Tess said, "Wait a minute. Remember that guy on the bus the other day who said your haircut was 'like beautiful, man'?"

"Yeah, but he was wearing a Raleigh Hills Outpatient wristband."

Cassandra laughed and poured herself more wine. "You two are cute together," she said. "Tess's energy is much lighter since you showed up. You've been a good influence on everybody."

Gabriel just rolled his eyes as Mr. Palmer said, "I have friends who believe that everyone we meet either stimulates or inhibits our spiritual growth."

Gabriel turned to Mr. Palmer. "I just wish being too good-looking really was my problem."

"Still," Mr. Palmer said mildly, "physical beauty might make you more self-involved, more judgmental, less inclined to see things from another's point of view. And if that were true, it could inhibit your full development in this lifetime."

"I don't want to be perfect, Mr. Palmer. Just not so skinny."

"You're fine, Gabriel. Very few fourteen-year-olds are content with their bodies. That's natural, and it will pass. Your real work lies elsewhere."

"What real work, my job?"

Mr. Palmer shook his head and patted the shirt pocket just above his heart. "In here."

"My real work is inside my chest?"

"It will reveal itself to you. It's revealing itself to you all the time." His smile went around the table, touching each of them like someone lighting candles, ending with Sumner.

"You're not going to tell me, are you." It wasn't even a question.

Cassandra smiled. "It's like gold, sweetheart—better if you discover it for yourself."

Mr. Palmer raised his water glass and took a sip. "I believe that nudism was a great stimulus for my personal growth. After a while, it was just skin, all of it, and desire took its natural place among the other passions." He smiled and looked around the table. "When I was Gabriel's age, of course, I thought if I ever saw an acre of naked ladies, I'd die on the spot from excitement. But later I did see them, and I didn't die. And out of them all, I chose Sunny, and she chose me." Then he looked down at the napkin in his lap, and both shoulders slumped.

An acre of naked ladies, thought Gabriel. Across the table Tess leered and waggled her eyebrows, and he scrunched up his face at her.

"Well," said Mona, "why don't we move into the living room . . ."

Tess glanced over her shoulder and said, "Not a journey we'll need faithful Sherpa porters for."

". . . and give these carbohydrates a chance to digest before we have dessert." Mona pretended to be stern with her daughter. "And maybe Ms. Smart Aleck will clean up in here."

"It's his fault," she said, pointing at Gabriel. "My energy is so much lighter now, I can't help but make spontaneous and devilishly clever remarks."

Gabriel stood up. "All right, all right. I'll help."

He stood at the sink and washed everything that Tess handed him. On the windowsill, nearly at eye level, stood one of those crystal globes with a pond inside made from a mirror no bigger than a watch crystal, plus a tiny church and two skaters not just holding hands but molded together. He knew that if he turned it upside down, snow would fall. He remembered being very small and watching his parents skate cross-handed on their own pond while he sat spraddled on a red Flexible Flyer sled and tried to catch snowflakes on his outstretched tongue.

Tess nudged him. "If you wash the pattern off that dish, my mom's going to be mad."

"Are we done then?"

"Yeah. Want to play a game or something?"

Gabriel dried his hands. In the living room, the grown-ups were talking. Cassandra had brought the bottle of wine from the table and was drinking out of it. "Sure," Gabriel said. "Which one?"

"Read My Lips?"

"Pardon me?"

"That's the name of the game—Read My Lips." She headed for the closet. "Sit down somewhere."

Sumner was in the middle of a sentence when Gabriel wandered by. ". . . and every morning I promise that that night we'll eat something really good for us, but by five o'clock, I'm tired or frustrated, and I end up micro-waving some monstrosity, or we go out and eat fast food." He rubbed his stomach. "But tonight I feel full and good, too."

"We should get you a steamer," Mona said, propping her bare feet on a small table with seashells arranged haphazardly under its glass top. "I remember the first time I ate fresh green beans I'd steamed myself. I thought I'd died and gone to heaven."

Gabriel settled on the floor at the end of the wicker couch. Mona's hand drifted over and settled on his head. "Your haircut's cute," she whispered.

"Back home it means you play for the Badgers."

"Here we go," Tess said, sitting down cross-legged opposite him. She unfolded a board with a curlycue path on it, set a small hourglass off to one side, stacked a tall deck of cards neatly, and held out four tiny pairs of lips, each a different color. "Pick one. It's your marker for when you move around the board, futilely pursuing me."

"Tess's father?" Mona said. "We met—as we say here in Hollywood—'on the set.' I was Leticia, leader of the Amazons, and he was washed ashore wearing little furry shorts." She shook her head and grinned. "Don't ask."

"You really need teams," Tess explained, "but this'll be okay." She held up a color-coded card. "I'm going to just move my lips, right? And say a person's name or a place or a saying or . . ."

"Mona was a very promising actress," Mr. Palmer said.

"Which means a lot of people made me a lot of prom-ises."

"But no whispering, okay?" Tess said. "And don't go 'buh' or 'duh' or 'ssst,' either. Make it like a silent movie."

"I wasn't that good an actress, anyway," Mona said.

Cassandra sounded sleepy: "With your moon in Jupiter, self-esteem will always be a problem for you."

Tess chose a card, and Gabriel watched her pink lips move soundlessly.

Mona sat up and ran both hands through her thick hair. "I could act a little, I guess, but then I'd see somebody really good, and it was like a light bulb looking at the sun and saying, 'Oh, that's how it's done.'"

"Morry's tuba?" Gabriel guessed.

"What?" Tess tapped the card. "Gabriel, it's a place. Morry's tuba is not a place."

"I'm just lucky I'm conventionally pretty," added Mona.

Gabriel glanced up at her, but she was engrossed in the conversation. Her remark, like all the others, floated over his head like wisps of clouds. He concentrated on Tess. Her tongue was as pink as her lips.

He insisted. "Morry's tuba could be a place. Like, 'Where's my lunch?' 'Oh, over by Morry's tuba.'"

Tess held up the hourglass with its blue sand. "The time is up, Columbus. It was Manitoba."

"Anyway," Mona said, "there was no way I was going to leave Tess alone, so I turned down parts that meant going on location or working sixteen hours a day, and I started making commercials. I'm just glad Mother isn't alive to see me and my sixteen years of dance lessons dressed like a Tater Tot."

"Every time I ask the universe about Mona," Cassandra announced, "I see thousands of people listening to her."

"Your turn," Tess said, shuffling the fat deck.

"Toby says that once I hit forty-five, I can put my hair in a French twist, look right into the camera, and say, 'When I'm troubled by occasional irregularity . . .'" She made a face. "I, for one, can hardly wait."

As Gabriel studied his card, Sumner asked, "Are you all native Californians?"

"Okay," Gabriel said, "this is a person." Tess nodded and stared at his mouth.

Mr. Palmer smiled. "I was born in South Dakota, which is not exactly nudist country."

"Hope!" Tess said. "Bob Hope!" She pounced on the plastic lips and bounced them along five spaces.

Cassandra said, "When I was a little girl, I'd tell my parents what I dreamed or saw, and when it came true they'd take me to the priest. So I just clammed up until I could get out of there. I'm not leaving L.A. until it's time for my next incarnation, which, if I'm lucky, will be as a catcher with the Astros."

Tess frowned at the board as Sumner's voice drifted past. "So you weren't born here, either?"

"Detroit," Cassandra said, "but I was drawn west, just like you were."

"Well?" said Gabriel as Tess thought.

". . . but I didn't come up with Timmy so I could take Hollywood by storm or even write a book. I made him up for Gabriel when he was little. Then he turned into a way for me to help my students learn to read; it just cracked them up when he pointed with his nose. It was only after that worked that I thought about writing down the stories I made up for Timmy to tell—you know, the flood, and when the tree fell down, and Sammy the Salmon, and all the rest of it." Sumner turned away from the window. "Maybe that's why it makes me so nuts when Miles wants to make *Tiny Timmy* for a Christmas special and then spends half an hour with one of his sycophants trying to decide if an otter could swim with a little crutch."

"Sumner, you're only here for a short while." Mona started across the room toward Cassandra, who'd nodded off in the flowered chair. "When the time's up, you simply tell them no changes. If they don't renew the option, you go home with Timmy intact."

Sumner looked pained. "But what if I don't want to go home? What if I like it here?"

Tess held up her card. "Really watch now, okay? This is a saying." She mouthed the words elaborately.

Gabriel guessed, "The chicken's fine?"

"What kind of saying is that?" she demanded.

Mona shook Cassandra. "Wake up," she said softly.

"Well, you take your chicken to the vet, leave it overnight, call up in the morning, and say, 'How's the chicken?' And the vet says, 'The chicken's fine.'"

"Don't get old if you can help it," Mr. Palmer said, holding on to Sumner's arm.

"Gabriel! It's a *popular* saying, one everybody knows like 'Birds of a feather flock together' or 'Look before you leap.' Whoever heard of 'The chicken's fine?'"

"I just had a wonderful dream," Cassandra said, rubbing her face with both hands. "It was fabulous. Full of mystery and portent. Wow."

"What about?" Mona asked.

She scratched her head, reaching up under the blue wool cap. "Gee, I forget."

"And I've forgotten," said Mr. Palmer, stretching and

grimacing, "what we did with the signs from last month's rally."

Tess looked up from the floor, where she was folding the colorful board.

"In our garage, I'm pretty sure."

"So what was the saying?" asked Gabriel.

Tess looked disgusted. "A stitch in time," she said deliberately.

"Well, I know this much," Cassandra grumbled. "It was about something."

"The protest is either the day after tomorrow," Mr. Palmer said, "or a week from the day after tomorrow."

Gabriel handed Tess the lid with all the colorful lips on it.

All of a sudden there were footsteps on the stairs, then the landing. Then the door swung open. There stood a dark-haired man wearing a turquoise tank top under a white suit. Not the kind an ice cream man wears though, or a TV evangelist, but a suit that moved when he moved and shimmered when he stood still.

He whispered, "Gotta go," into a cordless phone, then folded it up and dropped it into his jacket pocket. "Hi, everybody!" His teeth were so white they looked enameled.

"What brings you here, Desi?" Mona asked as if she already knew the answer.

He spread his arms wide, like an innocent man. "Maybe I was in the neighborhood. Maybe I just wanted to see my wife and kid."

Tess shot up from the floor. "I got stuff in the dryer!" She barged past her father's outstretched arm, snatched her camcorder off the table by the door, and was gone.

Mona put her hands on her hips and gave a little apologetic shrug. "Well, you know everybody but Sumner and Gabriel."

Desi's hand was out; his smile went from two hundred watts to two hundred and fifty. "Quarterback for the Rams named Gabriel once. You play?"

"Gee, I—" But Desi had already turned away. "Maybe Tess needs some help," Gabriel said to nobody in particular.

As he slipped out, he heard Desi say, "Sumner, huh? Catchy name. Your agent think that up?"

Gabriel paused on the stairs. The laundry room, a dozen yards away, was dark. He let his eyes adjust to the gloom, and then he saw Tess sitting by the lap pool with her back to him and everything else.

"You okay?" he asked, coming up on her slowly as if she might bite.

"What a jerk," she muttered.

Gabriel stood beside her, both hands in the back pockets of his jeans.

"Can I sit down?" he asked.

She scooted over maybe a thousandth of an inch. "Who does he think he is, anyway? Comes in like he owns the place, then just says he was in the neighborhood." She turned to Gabriel so fast the chaise wobbled. "You know what he wants, don't you?" she demanded.

Gabriel had wound a model plane so tight once that the whole thing just flew apart in his hand. Tess was like that—already quivering and liable to explode any minute. So he just shook his head.

She leapt to her feet. "Money! He only comes around when he wants money or—" Suddenly she kicked the nearest red-and-white chair toward the lap pool, then grimaced and hopped on one foot.

Upstairs a door opened; Gabriel heard Mona's voice and Desi's. Tess grabbed his arm and pulled him into the shadow of a fat palm. "Shhh." She pressed herself against Gabriel. Her hair smelled like something foresty—cedar, maybe. Or sandalwood. On the stairs, they could see only a pair of soft black shoes and two bare feet.

"I can't believe," Tess hissed, "he's dressed like he's still up for *Miami Vice*. That show's been in syndication for years."

The two sets of feet became legs, then torsos. When her parents kissed, Tess made a face. "Look at that. I can't believe her." Then she stalked away.

Impulsively, Gabriel picked up the camcorder. Tess was frozen in the foreground. Beyond her—part of her, in a way—were her folks: Desi's arm became her forehead, Mona's side the sweep of her nose.

Suddenly Desi turned away, whispered a good-bye, and took the last five steps in lighthearted bounds. Neither of them moved as he pecked a number into a tiny, portable phone, then disappeared into the foyer.

With a grunt, Tess launched the chaise into the lap pool. Startled, Gabriel put down the camera.

"Is this a terrible thing to say or what, but I can't help it. I hate my own dad."

"What'd he do?" Gabriel asked, stepping away from the splashing water. "I mean if you want to tell me."

Tess sniffed a couple of times, then spat into the grass. Gabriel could hear the gurgle of the pool filter and the hiss of cars on the distant freeway, a rasping sound like fine sandpaper on finished wood.

"He left us," she finally said into the darkness, "about a million years ago for some total zero with boobs out to here. I was just a little kid. I couldn't believe it."

"Did they get married?"

She shook her head and swabbed her face with the sleeve of her enormous T-shirt. "That one's history, and, anyway, he's still married to Mom, who is just as nice to him as she is to everybody else, and he doesn't deserve it!" Tess leaned over, put her head between her knees, and took two or three deep breaths. "Man, every time I see him I feel so weird."

Gabriel took a deep breath, too. "Look, I know exactly what you mean."

Tess, still resting one cheek on her knees, looked up at him. "You do?"

"Sure. You've seen my dad." He flattened one hand and made it dance around like Timmy. "And my mom . . . Don't get me wrong—I love her and all, but . . . well, Dad had barely moved out when she started dating." He shuddered. "She's off somewhere right now on her thousand-dollar mountain bike with some guy named Warren."

Tess sat up and took a swipe at her perfectly dry eyes with the palm of one hand. "Parents are something, aren't they?"

"No kidding." Gabriel stared almost straight up at the milky darkness. "And you know what kills me? I never get used to it. Not Mom's boyfriends. Not Timmy. I still get *so* upset. And then I feel guilty and creepy and mad and I don't know what-all." He pointed toward the condo. "Just before we came over to your place tonight,

Dad starts talking to me about something important, but *he's* not talking. That puppet is." He rubbed at his face with both hands. "I mean he almost always talks through Timmy, especially if he's nervous, and I know that, but it *still* gives me a stomachache."

Tess stood beside him and patted his stiff hair consolingly. She nodded toward her camcorder. "What'd you shoot?"

"Oh, just . . . I'm not sure. I mean, I didn't know what I was doing or anything, but you looked great sort of superimposed on your folks."

"Wow, really? Did you get like suppressed rage and total indignation?"

"I hope so. I don't know."

She reached for him impulsively, then drew her hand back. "It's just so cool that you did that. It's pure *Mondo Tess*."

Gabriel looked down at his hands, turning them this way and that as if they were brand new.

Then he followed her eyes toward the lap pool. "Maybe we ought to get that furniture out of there," she said, "before Mr. Palmer gets all tangled up in it tomorrow morning."

Gabriel grinned. He was glad to kneel down and drag the chair toward him through the tepid water. Then they worked together on the chaise, each taking an end, struggling to get it to the side as if it were the skeleton of some weird sea creature.

As they blotted their hands dry on their shirts, Tess glanced upstairs. Then she leaned to make sure the landing was empty and they were alone.

"I like talking to you," she said quietly. "Sure, I can quote share anything unquote with Mom, but this was better. We were really talking."

Gabriel whispered, too. "I know what you mean, and it did feel good. Like a relief. I mean I've got friends back home, like guys on the baseball team I'm tight with, but I don't think they'd understand stuff like this."

Just then a door opened upstairs. "Tess? Gabriel?"

"Down here, Mom."

"Will you make sure Mr. Palmer gets home all right?"

"C'mon." Tess turned to Gabriel. "I mean if you want to."

"Well, sure I want to," he said, taking her hand.

Mona's voice wafted downstairs. "Tess?"

She smiled at Gabriel. "We're coming, Mom."

Gabriel was sitting at the breakfast table by himself, staring at the spoon stuck in his oat bran. When he gave it a good pinging flick with his fingernail, it didn't move at all.

Just then the phone rang, so he crossed the kitchen—absently stepping on only the white tiles—answered it, and leaned against the wall.

"Hi!" said Tess. "What are you doin'?"

Eagerly he switched to his other ear. "Hi. I was just thinking about this dream I had. It was full of otters, so it was actually a nightmare."

"Well, don't tell Cassandra unless you've got about five hours to kill."

"Remember last week at dinner when Mr. Palmer said my work would be revealed to me?"

"Yeah?"

"What do you think he meant?"

"God, I don't know. He's always talking like that—they all do. As far as they're concerned, everything means something—nothing just happens. So I was *supposed* to get mad at my dad that night, and you were *supposed* to come to L.A."

"Yeah, but what for?"

"Beats me. What I want to know is what you did yesterday. I missed you." There was a pause. "I mean, I missed, you know, hanging out."

"Dad and I just went to about a thousand places. I wanted to leave a note, but he said it was Sunday and not to wake you guys up."

"So where'd you go starting at nine o'clock in the morning?"

"Mostly health food stores Mona turned him onto. Then we went clothes shopping on Melrose. He tried this dark brown suit on, kind of loose and free-flowing like your dad's, but he said it made him look like a mud slide."

Tess laughed. "Did he get anything?"

"The salesman told him he was an autumn, so he bought a turquoise shirt. What's an autumn, anyway?"

"It's just a way to match stuff to your eyes and skin and whatever. Everybody's one of the seasons."

"Which one are you?" he asked.

"I don't know. Mom told me, but I forgot."

"I'll bet you're a summer."

Gabriel listened to her breathe. *Maybe,* he thought, *I shouldn't have said that. Maybe she thinks I think she's hot.*

Finally she said, "Uh, want to do something?"

"Besides try to get my spoon out of some oat bran Dad made? Sure."

"Are you going to march with Mr. Palmer later at the cosmetics plant?"

"Are you?"

"If you are."

"Okay, good." Gabriel's ear was hot, so he blotted it against his shoulder.

"So, do you want to do something now? Like swim maybe?"

"I don't know if there's room. My dad's still down there with Mr. Palmer."

"I know. I can see them from here."

Gabriel slid along the wall till he reached the big windows. He pried the narrow blinds apart.

"God, he swims like a Saint Bernard."

"I saw his arms once, but then he sank."

"He says he's going to do laps every morning before work. He wants to lose a bunch of weight."

"Wait, I think they're getting out."

Gabriel watched Sumner crawl up the three steps that led out of the lap pool. "He looks pretty tired."

Mr. Palmer helped Sumner to his feet, then patted him on the shoulder. Then he demonstrated a stroke, his arms reaching slowly, his head turning to one side.

"Your dad is *so* white," Tess said. "I like it. He looks like an iceberg."

"He said yesterday your mom warned him to stay out of the sun."

They watched Sumner wrap himself up in a towel.

"Great, they're done. Meet you down there."

She hung up before Gabriel could say anything, much less no. So he trudged into the bedroom and dug out his trunks with BRADLEYVILLE P.E. on them.

Facing the mirror, he raised both arms and flexed. No muscle to speak of. Turning sideways, he tried to make his pectorals jump out the way the body builders on

ESPN did. Nothing. He felt thin as a book of poems. With a sigh, he slipped into a T-shirt.

Outside, he passed his father on the stairs.

"I almost drowned," Sumner panted. "Timmy would be ashamed of me."

"Timmy's watching *Wild Kingdom*, and I can keep a secret."

As Gabriel made his way across the artificial grass, which was already getting hot, he saw Tess spreading out a towel and dragging a couple of chaise lounges together. Two Cokes stood on the white table. When she spotted Gabriel, she grinned and waved.

Her swimsuit was blue and in one piece, like part of the sky in a jigsaw puzzle. It wasn't skimpy or revealing; it looked practical. And he'd seen almost all of her body, anyway, in shorts or tank tops. Still, it was different somehow. Gabriel figured he'd better get in the water in a hurry.

She beat him to it, just throwing herself backward into the narrow pool and coming up spluttering. She waved him in.

Gabriel crossed his arms self-consciously. He could count his ribs, like the narrow slats of a fence that kept his soul confined.

"I, uh, don't want to burn," he said.

"Leave your T-shirt on. And don't dive. It's too shallow."

Gratefully he jumped in. He'd no more than surfaced when Tess caromed water into his face and shoved him under again. This time he came up coughing and looking for revenge.

She was headed for the other end, so he struck out

after her, pumping hard, knowing she'd be trapped. But when he was almost up to her, she dove neatly under him—he felt her hair the whole length of his body—and was gone again.

This time she flattened herself against the side of the pool and let him thrash past, blinded by his own wake. Then she slipped away underwater again, leaving him looking around wildly. When he finally caught up, it was because she let him.

"Don't," pleaded Tess, both hands out like the grapplers on *Wrestle-Mania*. "I'm sorry I dunked you. I'll never do it again."

He let his tongue hang out dramatically. "God, maybe I ought to cut my dad some slack. This is tough."

"Are you really tired?" she asked.

"Are you kidding?"

"Exhausted?"

"Yes."

"Good!" She was on him again. Under he went, and the chase continued.

▼ ▼ ▼

An hour later, maybe more, they lay head-to-head beside the pool and dozed. Each let a hand dangle in the water. Their hair was almost touching.

Not far away, one of the Coke cans had fallen over. Tess opened one eye. "That'd make a kind of interesting shot," she said dreamily. "See how that white straw could be a rifle and the can is like a dead redcoat?"

"Where'd you learn so much about film, anyway?" he asked.

"It's all anybody ever talked about. When I was growing up, somebody was always coming over with a six-pack and a video. I must have seen *Citizen Kane* a hundred times."

"Did you ever like books, too?"

She shook her head. "Too slow."

"My mom read to me before I was even born and then every night for years." Gabriel wiped off one of the blue tiles, settled a fist on it, then balanced his chin on that. "Dad has these memories that just kill him, I guess. He and Mom'd be on the couch, right? And I'm like in her stomach still, and he'd put his head there, and then she'd put her hand on his head, and she'd read out loud."

"She sounds nice," Tess said.

"Did I tell you she was a sculptress?"

Tess reared, arching her back as if she were doing yoga or pretending to be a seal. "You're kidding."

"Nope."

"Wow, like Camille Claudel."

"Who's that?"

"Rodin's mistress. There's a movie about her." Tess reached for the remaining Coke. "How could she afford all that?"

"Her father left her some money when he died, and then she sold some pieces."

"I'll bet she was good."

Gabriel shrugged. "This one she donated to the library was called 'Mother and Child.' Everybody else called it 'The Doughnut.'"

"Did it look like one?"

"Exactly. A doughnut with a tumor. I got a little tired of being ragged about that."

"Well, my mom used to go to loonball retreats and I'd stay with the Palmers. Then she'd come back and drink out of different colored glasses for a month or make juice out of dirt."

"At least Mona got something out of it. She's healthy, and she looks great."

"Yeah, but your mom did something artistic."

Gabriel grinned. "Then she turned into a folk art collector."

"Like antiques?"

Gabriel tumbled sideways into the pool, as if even just thinking about his mother's weird phases had been enough to make him pass out.

"Worse," he said, surfacing and waiting until Tess sat up and put her feet in the water. "Chenille bedspreads and cornhusk dolls and these paintings where the Holy Ghost always looked like a big amoeba."

"What was your dad doing?"

"'Giving her room to grow,'" Gabriel quoted. "And working hard, you know? Like burying himself in it. He was Teacher of the Year once, for the whole state. And then he started to write. But he wasn't happy. Mom gets like obsessed. You know what I mean?"

Tess hooked her heels over Gabriel's shoulders and pulled him closer. He put his hands up to steady himself, each one closing over her bare, slippery ankles.

"Yeah," she said intently, "but Gabriel, at least then she was collecting art."

Gabriel gave her legs a playful tug, then mimicked her delivery. "Yeah, but Tess, your mom is in the movies. Mine made a two-thousand-pound doughnut."

"Hey, people in Brontosaurusville might think it's a doughnut, but what do they know about art? I'll bet Cassandra's right about your mom, that she's a restless soul.

Like me." Tess reached for some water and slicked back her hair. "That's what bothers me about Mona, I guess. She's happy in her little rut." She turned to Gabriel. "And she's not in the movies, either. She does ads."

"But she works for Toby, doesn't she? And you said the ads he makes are good."

Gabriel was about to say some more when he spotted something so unbelievable that he grabbed the edge of Tess's Spuds Mackenzie towel and wiped both eyes.

"When you ate breakfast this morning," he asked deliberately, "did you put everything away afterward?"

Tess had her eyes closed, head thrown back. "I don't know. Why?"

"'Cause an ant just came out of the foyer."

Tess snorted. "What do I care about *an* ant."

"This one's about five-seven."

Tess whirled to her left. "Oh, my God," she said, letting her head fall forward melodramatically as the ant headed their way, its middle legs bouncing.

"Hi, guys," Mona said. Her face was shiny with coal-colored makeup; she had huge round segments covering her shoulders and hips, black tights, long black gloves, coiled antennae that bounced, and enormous eyelashes. "This makes your dad your uncle," she said to Tess, "which makes you my niece, too." She had her real arms akimbo on her lower, balloony segment. "Get it—ant, uncle?"

"Very funny, Mom."

"What's going on here, anyway?" she asked. "It's almost twelve. I had Toby bring me right home the minute we were through." She looked around, antennae dancing. "Where are the posters? You were supposed to get them out of the garage."

"We'll get 'em, Mom. Just please go upstairs and take off that stupid costume."

"I thought I might picket in it. You know—Insects for Animal Rights." She cocked her head. "Of course it'd be better if I were dressed like a flea."

"Let me guess: bug spray commercial?" Gabriel asked, shading his eyes.

"Uh-huh." Mona raised her arms gracefully and let them flutter down. "I got to die."

"She trains for *Swan Lake*," Tess pointed out, "and ends up doing *Ant Hill*."

"Just wait till the residuals buy you some school clothes." Mona raised one black-gloved hand to her enormous eyes. "And where's Mr. Palmer? This is his show."

"Asleep," Tess and Gabriel said in unison.

Mona shifted her top segment, then looked at Tess. "Too bad your dad's not here. Fifty-six, twenty-three, fifty-six are his kind of measurements."

"Only the first fifty-six," Tess pointed out.

Mona looked down, inspecting her bulbous body, then grimaced. "Wow, I have to take these lashes off or I'm going to get muscles in my eyelids."

Gabriel and Tess watched her scurry away.

"You don't think that's weird?" Tess demanded.

"A little, I guess. But nowhere near as weird as you-know-who."

"Oh, bull. Your dad's fine."

"Looks like we should switch parents."

Then they grinned at each other as Tess took her right

foot off Gabriel's shoulder and, as if it were her hand, rubbed it against his cheek.

"I'm really glad you came out here this summer," she said.

That's when he reached for her foot and kissed it. He didn't think or plan. He just did it. And afterward he thought he was going to faint.

But not just from embarrassment. That he covered up by sinking slowly into the pool. By disappearing. He thought he might faint from the way it felt—her soft, clean skin against his lips.

When he surfaced, his heart was thudding. Tess stared at him, her lips parted, breathing hard, too. He still held her left foot—pinker at the heel, pale at the toes, each one lit by polish, making a row of torches. When she wiggled them—not drawing away, though—Gabriel felt like he was falling out of his body.

Tess's voice was husky and low. "Maybe we should go out to the garage and look for those posters."

Though she was barely wet at all anymore, Tess wrapped a long towel around her waist as they set out, so Gabriel did, too. They looked foreign then. Exotic. Like people from Java or Bali.

Gabriel picked his way gingerly through the construction site—a shattered two-by-four here, nails bent into L's there—and then across the wide asphalt drive that ran in front of all the garages.

The blacktop hurt his feet, but no way was he going to stop and tiptoe upstairs for his flip-flops. Second of all, it was just too dorky to say, "Oh, wait. My little feet can't stand this!" But more important than that, there was something mysterious and wonderful going on. And Gabriel knew deep down that this spell, this peculiar and sudden happiness, could shatter and disappear like a window of ice.

They skirted Mona's old VW wagon, then lifted the big garage door a few feet and ducked under, leaving it propped halfway like a stifled yawn.

Inside it was like every garage Gabriel had ever seen. Messy cans of paint sat on makeshift shelves; cardboard cartons were stacked until they leaned precariously. There was a girl's bike with a flat tire, a box from some veterinarian with a picture of a cat in a wheelchair. The farthest corner had sprouted a stand of handles, some round like broomsticks, some with corners, and all tacked to big pieces of poster board.

And there was a couch. A beige one with one broken leg so that it slanted like a pinball game. Gabriel looked at Tess, and she looked back.

"It's our old one," she said softly, leaning against him so imperceptibly that only their knotted towels touched. "It broke. My folks broke it."

Gabriel felt the whole soles of his feet on the cool concrete; the tongues of paint on the Sherwin-Williams cans leapt out at him; the air was rich enough to write on. He could hear Tess moving behind him, the sound her dry lips made parting, the suck of flesh one bare arm made as it left her brow.

"We could sit down," he said. "For a minute."

"Yeah, we'd better rest up. Those signs are pretty heavy." She gave a throaty little bark that passed for a laugh.

Gabriel grinned back and swallowed hard. He was *so* dry.

"Tess!" It was Mona's voice, from the other world. "Tess?"

Tess grabbed his forearm to steady herself. Gabriel groaned and took—tried to take—a deep breath. Then he harvested a handful of placards and passed some to Tess, stirring up the dust.

▼ ▼ ▼

Twenty minutes later, Gabriel, Sumner, and Timmy were waiting for Mr. Palmer to make his way toward the foyer when Cassandra shot out of her apartment carrying a folded beach chair and a small Igloo cooler.

"I'm not going," she cried. "I can't go."

"Why not?" demanded Timmy, waggling his whiskers.

"Because I have to be here today." She pointed with her green-and-white chair. "Or out there, anyway. On the corner."

"Ready?" Mona said, coming into the courtyard from out front, where she'd moved her car.

"Cassandra's not coming," Sumner said.

Gabriel peered around Mona and caught Tess's eye. "Hi," he said softly.

She smiled back. "Long time no see."

"I had this dream," Cassandra said, opening the foyer door and nodding to Gabriel to hold it for her. "Unbelievably vivid, down to the last detail. And I remember everything!" She walked backward, filling the others in as they followed.

"Right there," she exclaimed, turning as they came out in the sunlight, "on that corner, a child in a red raincoat will be killed by a speeding automobile unless I'm here to prevent it."

Timmy looked up at the sky. "A raincoat?"

"The rodent's right," Gabriel said. "There's not a cloud in the sky."

Timmy looked at Sumner. "Five years since he's said one word to me, and then it's an insult!" The puppet glared at Gabriel. "I'm not a rodent!" he insisted. "I'm a mammal."

"Dreams don't lie," Cassandra said. "You all go on. Just look for me on the news tonight: Prominent Psychic Saves Child."

As she hurried away in her green muumuu, cooler in one hand, chair in the other, Timmy said, "She looks like a shrub on its way to the beach."

Sumner reprimanded Timmy as they settled into the car—he and the otter in front with Mona; Gabriel, Tess, and Mr. Palmer in the back. As they drove, the handles of the placards chattered in the rear of the station wagon.

"Scooch this way," Tess said. "Give Mr. Palmer some room."

Gabriel slid right up next to her. His left arm went around the back of the seat, but he didn't know what to do with the other one. So he smoothed his black twills. "I, uh, didn't know exactly what to wear to a protest," he said. "I figured nothing too cheerful."

"You look great," Tess said.

"Not as good as you."

She waved the compliment away. "I wear just about the same thing every day."

"So? You look great every day."

"You're fine, Gabriel," Mona said without turning around. "The dress code is pretty loose, except it's probably best to not show up in a lot of leather."

"Because leather jackets come from animals, right?" Gabriel said.

"Right. It's a little weird to see some guy in eight yards of cowhide screaming about being cruel to white rats."

Sumner had Timmy pressed up against the window on his side, waving at startled drivers in the adjoining lanes, but he turned away to ask how long Mona had been actively protesting for animal rights.

"Oh, on and off for years. Mr. Palmer got me interested. When Tess started school, I had a lot of time on my hands, and I tended to brood. He helped me stop thinking about myself all the time."

Everyone in the car looked at Mr. Palmer, who had dozed off.

"Does it help to protest?" asked Timmy. "I sure hate to think about my pals in there with blusher on their butts."

Mona took her eyes off the road for an instant. "Maybe it's best not to make jokes, Sumner. Some of us take this very seriously."

To break the uncomfortable silence, Gabriel finally asked, "But it does help, doesn't it?"

"You know," Mona said evenly, "it does. More and more all the time I see disclaimers on products that say, 'Not Tested on Animals.' I don't think that would've ever happened if somebody hadn't raised a stink about it."

"Do people do really cruel things?" Gabriel asked.

"I'm afraid so."

As the big yellow Arrowhead Water truck ahead of

them stopped, Mona braked hard and began to glance in her rearview mirror for an opening.

"Are you a vegetarian?" Gabriel whispered to Tess.

"Pretty much."

"Because your mom is?"

She shook her head. "No, I thought about it, and it seems cruel—I mean all that killing just so I can have a hamburger."

Gabriel frowned out the window. "I'll bet nobody in Bradleyville is a vegetarian. About half the guys go out and shoot Bambi every November and then drive around with him tied to their fenders."

"Not your dad."

"For sure not."

"Hunting is gross. I mean it."

He leaned closer to whisper. "You don't think it's like hypocritical for me to march today without feeling really strong about this stuff yet, do you?"

Tess shook her head decisively. "Uh-uh. Maybe it'll help you decide."

"It's not like I'm in favor of cruelty or anything. It's just that I've never really thought about . . ."

She linked their fingers. "I know. Don't worry. It's okay."

Then Tess twisted around in the seat and got on her knees facing the back. Gabriel heard her fussing with the signs, so he turned around, too. As the car swayed or changed lanes, their shoulders rubbed.

"I'm picking one out for you," Tess said. "I'm between No Blood for Superficial Beauty and Even White Mice Have Rights."

"Why don't you take one, and I'll take the other?"

She shook her head. "I need a crowd scene for *The Big Nap*. Then I'll shoot some *Mondo Tess*, I hope."

Tess reached for her camcorder as a Volvo ducked in behind them. The driver was talking on his car phone and, on the other side of the baby seat, his wife was dialing another one.

Tess used up ten seconds of film. "Too good to pass up," she said. "Quintessential L.A. Do you know what that means?"

"Sure, Los Angeles."

She grinned and bumped her hips against his. "I meant *quintessential*."

"The best? Ultimate?"

"See, you're not just cute—you're smart, too."

Gabriel felt himself begin to glow. "Oh, sure."

As Mona angled into the right lane toward a freeway exit, Gabriel and Tess turned around. When they bounced back into their seats and fumbled for their belts, Mr. Palmer stirred. "Sunny?" he said.

Tess leaned across Gabriel. "We're almost there, Mr. Palmer. Time to wake up."

As they glided onto a quiet street, Tess pointed her camera out the window.

"The neat cottages," she narrated under her breath, "made Elvis Miyata's skin crawl. Where the average citizen saw windows, Elvis saw the empty eyes of rotting skulls."

"That's it down there," Mona said, leaning forward to squint at a tall white building with lots of glass.

"It looks like any corporate office," Sumner said.

"The decaying edifice," Tess muttered, "loomed into the filthy sky, shutting out even the feeble sun's pitiful attempts at illumination."

Mona put on her sunglasses as she coasted into a parking place. "Let's go to work, guys."

They trooped up the street toward the main entrance, where there were already thirty or forty people milling around.

"What now?" Gabriel asked. "Do we have to yell or anything?"

"We just walk around," Mona said. "If we get lucky and it's a slow news day, a TV crew comes by."

"So, they know we're here."

"Oh, sure. Mr. Palmer used to be in charge of all that—letters to the media, phone calls, news releases, follow-ups, you name it."

Gabriel glanced over his shoulder at Mr. Palmer, who was leaning on his sign. "Why did he stop?"

Mona smiled. "He got tired, honey."

As her mom turned away, Tess closed in on Gabriel. "Elvis," she narrated, "should have known he could never blend in with such a motley crew. His skin glowed with perfect, robust, masculine health, a stark contrast to the pasty complexions of the hummus-chomping do-gooders all around him. His full, sensuous lips were like rubies."

"Holy cow, Tess."

She lowered the camera. "Under the circumstances, that's 'Holy carrots,' and try to act natural."

Gabriel marched along with the others. Occasionally passing cars would honk, and he learned to wave his placard, too, acknowledging their support. As he made the sharp turn at the end of each block, he could take in the other people: young couples in Birkenstocks, middle-aged people in light windbreakers or sweaters, some older folks in stretch pants and comfortable shoes. There were lots of babies slung across their parents' chests or backs. A few people wore beaded headbands.

Mona cruised up beside him. "Everything okay?" she asked.

"Sure."

"Not like Bradleyville, though, huh?"

"Thank goodness."

Mona grinned. "Do you like L.A. better?"

He glanced around for Tess and found her high on the white steps, looking down through her viewfinder. "I like some things about it a lot."

"It's a funny place." She pointed to a small tree with tiny leaves. "Olive," she said. "Almost the only indigenous tree. Everything else was brought in."

"Like me."

"Like most of California."

Now Tess was lying on her back in the grass nearby, shooting straight up at the Colombo Cosmetics building.

"What do they really do in there, anyway?" he asked.

"Well, the labs at this location are in the back, as far from the street as they can get them. And basically they use animals to see if any of their products could maybe blind a customer or make her skin break out."

Gabriel stopped, and other marchers parted around him like water. "They blind animals?"

"One hopes not very often." Then she tugged at Gabriel, drawing him off to one side. "Let's wait for the others."

Glancing around, he saw a uniformed guard saunter out of the big double doors, walk toward them, and pause at the top of the stairs.

"Can we get you folks to stay off the grass, please?" he shouted amiably. "We just seeded down there, and we want to give it a chance to grow. Thanks."

"With the cacophonous shrieks of mutilated beasts in the background," Tess hissed, "hired thugs stormed out of the building, truncheons at the ready. Elvis knew he was in for a fight, but he welcomed it. His steely fists ached to send snakes of pain slithering through their tiny brains."

"You've got some imagination, Tess," Gabriel said.

"All artists do."

"Are you okay?" said Mona as Mr. Palmer stumbled out of line toward her and the others.

"Just a little tired, Mona," he said, panting. "I'll be all right in a minute."

As Sumner began to fan him with his sign, a white van pulled up at the curb, and a wiry-looking man with amber-tinted sunglasses hopped out. With both hands on his hips as if he were about to lead an aerobics class, he took everything in.

Then he snapped an order to the driver and jogged their way. His blue-and-white exercise outfit made the same kind of rustling sound as the palm fronds outside Gabriel's bedroom window.

"Can I get you all back in line?" he said. Then his hand landed on Mr. Palmer's shoulder. "How about it, Pop? Are we in or out here?"

"He's just resting," Mona said sharply.

"Fine." He pointed. "Rest over there out of camera range, okay?" And he gave Mr. Palmer a polite shove.

That's when Sumner's sign—the one that said DON'T BE CRUEL—hit the man on the head, knocking his sunglasses askew.

Timmy opened his arms wide, showing his white paws. "Sorry," he squeaked. "It slipped."

The man leaned over and snatched at his Cybervision glasses angrily. "Who are you people, anyway?"

"The question is," Mona answered, "who are *you*? I've never seen you before."

He glanced at his watch, which was very thick, as though he might have to tell time underwater any minute. "I'm Mel Reynolds. I'm from the East Coast, and I'm out here to get this movement back on its feet."

"Not feet," Timmy insisted. "Paws!"

As Gabriel cringed, Mel looked at him sympathetically.

"They told me about L.A.," he growled half to himself, "but, oh, no, I wouldn't believe them." Then he turned to Mona. "I've got Channel Seven due here anytime, lady. And a march in San Pedro to make by five." Then he took his glasses off, revealing gray eyes. He rubbed at the bridge of his nose. "So the old guy's gotta keep up."

"It's not 'the old guy'; it's *Mr.* Palmer," Mona said.

Mel turned. "Not Pete Palmer."

"Yes."

He seized Mr. Palmer's hand and shook it. "My God, you're a legend. Sorry, you know, about coming on too strong. I used to hear about you in Jersey."

Mr. Palmer stood up a little straighter. "Longevity, I imagine. More than merit."

"Whatever. It's a pleasure to meet you; I thought you were—" He stopped abruptly, cocked one ear, then turned. "Here comes the mobile unit."

"If I might suggest," Mr. Palmer began, "we have a prominent author of children's books here, and—"

"Pete, you're a free agent. You do what's best for your people. I gotta go."

Timmy appeared over Mr. Palmer's shoulder, and the old man raised his left hand and scratched the otter's head.

"I've noticed if you're twenty-five," Mr. Palmer said, "you have an opinion. If you're seventy-five, you're in the way. God help you if you're ninety."

"He's a jerk," Mona said. She turned to Sumner. "I liked it when you bopped him one with your sign."

Sumner looked at the ground. "It was my way of apologizing," he murmured, "for what I said earlier, what I had Timmy say, I mean. When I get nervous, I talk too much."

As her mom linked arms with Sumner, Tess said, "Did you see how hairy his hands were? I'm surprised he came in a van. He could've made better time through the trees."

Mr. Palmer smiled a little but shook his head, too. "Now, now," he cautioned. "Being unkind won't help. Let's all join in and swell the ranks." He pointed toward a large sycamore tree. "If you'll go along, I'll join you shortly." He patted his white cotton poncho with the deep pouch. "I have some orange sections here. I just need to rebalance my blood sugar."

Gabriel hung back a little as everyone else filed away.

"Are you sure," he asked, "that you'll be okay? I don't mind sitting with you. I'm a little tired, too."

"No, no. I'll be fine. You go and walk beside Tess, all right? I like to see the two of you together."

▼ ▼ ▼

"Do you think he's okay?" Sumner asked, twisting around in the bucket seat to peer at Mr. Palmer, who was asleep.

"It was a long day," Mona said, leaning on the horn as a Mustang convertible cut in front of her. Then she glanced at her right shoulder, where Timmy was curled up. "Everybody's tired."

"I'm not tired," Tess whispered to Gabriel. "Are you?"

"Uh-uh."

"Good. 'Cause we've got chores to do when we get home, like put the signs back in the garage and stuff."

Gabriel put his arm around the back of the seat. "Yeah, that's right."

It was just after six, and the freeway was like some futuristic ghetto where everyone lived side by side in glassed-in, colored cocoons. Gabriel watched a man lean toward his rearview mirror and floss, a young woman in a perky red beret and huge beads put on more makeup, and a carful of commuters pass around a flat box of pizza.

"One time when I was gridlocked," Mona said, "some guy got out of his pickup, ran across the top of a bunch of cars, jumped into the oleanders, and disappeared."

"I have to admit that I miss being able to go anywhere in about ten minutes," Sumner said.

"What a whiner," Mona kidded him. "We went at least ten feet in the last ten minutes."

"What do you miss about home?" Tess whispered to Gabriel.

"Not much. The weather, maybe." He glanced outdoors at the enormous parfait of smog: murky greens, yellows, and browns. And above it all, like a dirty meringue, what passed for a cloud. "This is a little postnuclear for me."

She turned into the curve of his arm. "Anything else?"

"Sounds, I guess, especially the ones at night. You know—stuff like crickets and owls and wind in the trees."

"But just things. There's nobody you miss a lot."

He turned toward her more. "The air may not be very good, but I'm crazy about the people in L.A."

Just then Mona saw her chance and darted across two lanes, making a Mercedes brake sharply. The driver—a weary-looking young woman in a blue power suit—flipped her off halfheartedly.

"Makes being a dancing ant look like a wise career move," Mona said, taking the off-ramp at Lincoln.

When they were a block or so from home, Sumner leaned forward, wiping at the glass. "I think I see Cassandra." He pointed. "Isn't that her still sitting out there?"

Mona took her foot off the gas and coasted past the other huge apartment buildings—the Lanai, the Berkshire Arms, Villa del Mar, and Versailles.

"Maybe," she said. "We better go see. Look, Tess, I'll pull up by the drive, and you and Gabriel—"

"Okay!"

Mona glanced in the tiny mirror. "Okay, what?"

"Okay, you pull up by the drive, and we'll hop out and put the signs away while you guys go check out Cassandra."

Gabriel could see Mona's eyes narrow in the rearview mirror: "I was going to say I'll pull up, and you and Gabriel help Mr. Palmer and then go see if Cassandra's all right. There's no point in three of us bumping into each other in that little garage."

"But, Mom, I think it'd be better if—"

Mona's knuckles got pale against the black steering wheel. "Will you just please do what I want for once?"

Tess stiffened. "For once?" she echoed. "God, all I ever do is what you want. What about *me* for once? What about what *I* want? Why does everybody else come first, huh? Cripes, I'm your daughter!"

It was quiet in the car. Sumner silently squeezed Timmy's lips shut so he wouldn't blurt anything out. Finally Mona, sounding super-controlled, said, "It's been a long day. We'll talk about this later. But for right now"—she left huge spaces between each word—"help Mr. Palmer."

A few minutes later, everyone but Mona was standing around Cassandra's aluminum chair. At their feet, empty beer cans lay scattered like bowling pins.

"Almost dark," said Sumner.

Cassandra scowled. "And when it's completely dark, I'll give up, but not before."

Mr. Palmer knelt and slowly began to put the empty cans back into Cassandra's blue Igloo cooler. Timmy hung upside down at Sumner's side, like a bat.

"Did you see any children at all?" Sumner asked. "Even without red raincoats?"

Cassandra's old Keds dug in as she pushed herself up straighter in her chair. "Of course I saw children. They just weren't exactly in red."

"They were in raincoats, though."

"Well, maybe they were in shirts." She turned to glare at Sumner. "But long shirts."

"Red shirts?"

"Nearly. They were, uh, yellow."

"You got sunburned," Mona said, joining the others. "You should have worn a bigger hat."

Tess looked up at the sky. It was the color of purple chalk, the kind that children use to draw on blackboards.

"No rain, either," she whispered to Gabriel.

"I heard that!" Cassandra snapped.

"There's still time," Gabriel pointed out. "Or almost, anyway."

Mona put both hands on Cassandra's shoulders. "Come inside now. You've had a lot to drink."

Accordionlike, Cassandra collapsed in her chair. "I'm so disappointed," she whimpered. "I could have sworn . . ."

Just then a low mutter in the background turned into a rhythmic throbbing and then into a finely tuned roar. Everybody looked down the street as a black low-slung sports car powered toward them, tried to make the turn at Sycamore Street, and skidded into the curb, where it bounced and ran over the squat red hydrant. Immediately water geysered skyward, falling just a few yards from where Cassandra sat surrounded by her friends.

"See!" she shouted, leaping to her feet triumphantly. "Rain!"

▼ ▼ ▼

Next morning at breakfast, Gabriel got up twice to look out the window.

"What are you two doing today?" Sumner asked, sounding glum.

Gabriel automatically said, "Going to the movies." Then he turned. "How did you know I was looking for Tess?"

"Who else?" Sumner reached for a honey container shaped like a bear, pointed the nozzle down at his cereal, then didn't squeeze but stared at it instead and put it back.

"Let me guess," Gabriel said, sitting down again. He was in a good mood, remembering yesterday with Tess. "Bobo the Bear, right? And the story's about how he's afraid people don't like him for himself, just for what comes out of his hat."

"Actually I was thinking about that stupid thing I said on the way to the rally, and how Mona got mad at me." He clutched his spoon, most of the handle buried in his fist, like an enormous, hungry child. "I'm ashamed of myself. My God, here I am among people with strong convictions, people who are doing something unselfish and kind, and all I can do is make jokes about a bunny's butt."

"But you apologized—I heard you. And Mona didn't stay mad."

Sumner, dressed for work in a new purple shirt—with a paper napkin tucked in at the neck—acted as though he hadn't heard a word. "The funniest thing happened last night," he said, putting down his spoon and picking up a pair of chopsticks. "It was about eleven, and I couldn't sleep, so I thought I'd just go out for a breath of fresh air. And the next thing I know I'm walking straight to Cassandra's, and she's sitting there with her front door open like she knew I was coming."

110

"Dad, she always leaves her door open when it's hot."

Sumner toyed with a piece of apple, finally giving up and laying the chopsticks across Timmy, who was folded like a napkin near his plate.

"I found myself telling her that California wasn't what I expected, that I wasn't happy after all. Then I told her it wasn't just the studio or the city, but it was me, too." He looked directly at his son. "Guess what she said? 'You can't move on until you have the highest regard for where you are now.'" He spread his hands wide. "Now, what do you think that means?"

"Tess says everybody around here talks in riddles like that."

"I never thought much about having any particular regard for who I am. I thought I was just me, Sumner, and that was that."

"Dad, she can't tell a kid from a fire hydrant."

"Mona told me Cassandra was really something once. Movie stars came to see her, and politicians and investors—all kinds of important people. Then she started drinking, or at least drinking a lot more. By the time she moved to the Harmony Arms, she didn't have many clients left."

Gabriel frowned. "She's hammered about half the time, if you ask me."

"Mona says to not let that fool you." Then he rubbed his smooth, round face with both hands. "You know what? When Mona got mad at me in the car, it reminded me of all the times I acted out with Timmy and made your mother mad."

"Mona's a lot easier-going than Mom," Gabriel observed.

"There's nothing wrong with your mother." Sumner sounded stern.

"I didn't say there was. But, c'mon, admit it—compared to Mom, Mona's not so intense."

Sumner shifted in his chair. "I suppose I know what you mean."

Gabriel stood up and carried both cereal bowls to the sink. "Do you like Mona? I mean as in really like?"

"Mona's a good friend who has a husband."

"Some husband," Gabriel muttered. Then he turned around to face his father. "That Desi guy is kind of a creep."

"Why do you say that?"

"Are you kidding? He just left her and his daughter to go off with somebody else."

"Nice people do that, even if it isn't a nice thing to do."

"*And* he borrows money from her all the time. That's why he came by that night."

"Who told you that?"

Gabriel heard Tess's footsteps on the concrete stairs. "Gabriel?" she called from outside. "Are you ready?"

He pointed through the closed door. "Tess told me."

"Well," Sumner said, "she might have assumed that, but—" At Tess's rapid, woodpecker's knock, Sumner called out, "He's coming!" Then he met his son's eyes and held them. "But those aren't exactly the facts."

▼ ▼ ▼

Cutting across the tiny lawn in front of the Harmony Arms, Gabriel watched two workers in orange coveralls and hard hats struggle with a new hydrant.

"Is Cassandra ever right?"

Tess adjusted her painter's hat with GLIDDEN on the

112

tiny bill. "Why? Did she tell you something you want to believe?"

"More Dad than me, I guess. It's not like I'm banking on having broad shoulders by dinnertime."

Tess pushed back the bill of her hat. "The last time I remember her being absolutely right on the money was when everybody else was moving out of the Harmony Arms and she said to just wait, because the work would no more than get started than the money would run out and she and Mr. Palmer and Mom and I could stay on."

"Which happened, right?"

"Yeah, like one time out of twenty-five, maybe. You can get that with a dart board."

As they waited on the corner, Gabriel turned around and stared up at the nearest apartment building, a big pink place called the Double Tree Arms. People glided past plate glass windows like fish in an aquarium. They headed left, then right, then left again. One couple stopped and waved their arms; another exchanged brief, decaffeinated kisses.

Tess tugged at his hand as the light changed. Gabriel glanced at her hoping she wanted to hold his hand and not just hurry him along.

Halfway across the street, he asked, "Did Desi really come over to borrow money the other night?"

She leaned forward to check for the bus. "Why?"

"Oh, Dad and I were talking about, you know, stuff. And something he said sounded like you weren't right about Desi taking any money."

Tess looked down at her black canvas shoes with L.A. GEAR written all over them. "Well, maybe not last time, but lots of times before. And anyway, the money he gave her was ugly. He'd been out by Indio working on some schlock film called *Cult of the Cave Babes*. Can you believe that? I wouldn't buy toilet paper with money like that."

Gabriel frowned a little. "Is that really any worse than getting thirty thousand dollars for *Timmy the Otter?*"

"Are you kidding? Timmy's sweet."

"A cave full of girls doesn't sound that bad to me. Maybe they're all valedictorians."

"In fur bras? I doubt it." Tess whipped off her glasses and wiped the lenses vigorously on her T-shirt with IN-TERVIEW scrawled across it.

"Are we, uh . . ." Gabriel hesitated.

"What?"

"Are we really going to the movies?"

She cocked her head at him. "Sure. Where else?"

"Nowhere. I was just checking."

They sat there for a few minutes, each pretending to watch the traffic. Once a car went by with a child's face framed in the window, reminding Gabriel of a locket his mom had, which opened up to reveal his tiny photograph.

When their bus came, Tess darted ahead. Gabriel paid, then settled into the narrow seat, glancing at the names scratched into the scratchproof metal all around him.

He looked over at a preoccupied Tess. Was she even going to talk about what they'd felt in the garage yesterday?

He heard the camcorder go on. "I like it when you're moody," she said.

"I'm not moody. I was just thinking."

"What about?" she asked.

"I guess I was thinking about what you were thinking."

She let the camcorder slide off her shoulder. "I was thinking about you."

He turned eagerly. "Yeah?"

"Uh-huh. I was hoping you'd like *From Here to Eternity.*"

"Oh."

"If you do, we could go tomorrow, too. The Mayan is having a Montgomery Clift film festival this whole week."

Gabriel nodded. So she wasn't going to talk about the garage, after all. Well, maybe it hadn't happened. Maybe he was the only one whose heart was pounding when he saw that couch. Maybe when she'd argued with her mom in the car, it really was about those stupid posters.

"Gabriel?"

He shook his head. "Sorry. What?"

She looked mildly exasperated. She spoke extra-slow, as if he'd just scored a two on the last comprehension quiz. "If you like this movie, there's more next week."

"I know. I know. With Montgomery Clift, whoever he is."

"I love Montgomery Clift." She glanced around, then leaned and whispered, "He was probably asexual."

Gabriel's ear felt hot. "A sexual what?"

"*Non*sexual, like *a*political means not political."

"Oh." *So she loves people who aren't sexual.*

"Did you ever see *The Misfits?*"

"It's the story of my dad's life."

She gave him an elbow in the ribs. "It was Marilyn

Monroe's last movie. We could see it this weekend if you want."

Gabriel rubbed his side. So it *was* going to be business as usual. The garage really hadn't happened, at least not the way he thought. Great—now he was nuts, too.

"Gabriel?"

"Sure. *The Misfits* this weekend. I was listening."

The bus wound down Los Feliz and cruised through Hollywood, which always seemed to Gabriel like the center for fast food. Tess never ate there, but she really loved the Chicken Boy. Standing on a flat roof between a sleazy lingerie shop and a drugstore was a twenty-foot youngster in jeans, a checkered shirt, and a chicken's head, complete with a beak and a red comb.

When she leaned across him to stare, Gabriel automatically put his arm around her. "Look," he said, pointing out the other window where, directly opposite, Big Chicken Little had a handlettered sign in their window: CHICKEN BOY EATS HERE.

"Answers the question," Gabriel said, "Why does Chicken Boy cross the road?"

Tess sat up, grinning, and pulled his arm around her tighter, keeping it there until it was time to get off the bus. Confusing him thoroughly.

Gabriel shielded his eyes from the glare as Tess pointed proudly at the towering facade of the Mayan. "It's like really old," she said, "and was going to be torn down or made into one of those triplex shoe box things until a bunch of us wrote letters and called our city councillors and stuff."

Gabriel took in the carved stone front with its

compressed-looking serpents and birds, as if they'd been stacked for storage. A marquee advertised A WEEK OF MONTGOMERY CLIFT.

The lobby was musty and cool, with fifty years of Milk Duds ground into the carpet. It felt like a garage to Gabriel, but he tried to forget that as they stood in line for popcorn and Cokes.

Inside, he let Tess choose seats toward the back. The place was really enormous. There were murals on every wall, mostly muscular-looking Aztecs wearing headdresses and holding virgins who'd fainted. The light came from make-believe torches fitted with red bulbs.

As the music started, Tess whispered, "Do you like to ration your munchies so they last through the movie or just pig 'em right down?"

"Either way is okay with me."

"Let's make them last."

The movie turned out to be pretty good. It was about these soldiers based in Hawaii just before Pearl Harbor. There were friendly prostitutes in it and those brawls where someone gets hit with two or three tables and in the next scene has a little tiny cut on his forehead.

Tess knew some of the dialogue by heart, muttering right along with Donna Reed or Deborah Kerr. Every now and then she'd whisper, "Watch how cool this next shot is."

Gabriel's mind wandered, though, because Tess leaned into him a lot and their buttery hands were forever meeting in the jumbo box of popcorn.

Then there was this scene on the beach where Burt Lancaster, who was just a sergeant or something lowly like that, was making out with classy Deborah Kerr. It lasted a long time because they got sand everywhere and had to wait for the tide to come in and wash them off.

Tess stopped eating and talking. She just stared at the screen and licked her lips. Gabriel felt hot all over, as if he'd contracted malaria just from watching a film about the tropics.

"Tess?"

He hoped she knew what that one word meant, which was "I don't know what to do." And "Don't make fun of me if I'm wrong." And "Please."

She seemed to understand, because she turned right into him and they kissed. Involuntarily, Gabriel moaned.

"Are you okay?" she whispered when they finally stopped.

He glanced at his left hand. "Yeah, but I think my Coke's on fire."

"Wow." She fell back.

"No kidding." Dazed, he stared at the screen where everybody was wearing helmets. How long had that kiss lasted?

"Tess? Let's get out of here."

"But it's not over."

"I think we should go back home and check on those signs. Maybe your mom didn't put them away right."

She straightened her T-shirt. "Oh, yeah. Those are good signs. We wouldn't want anything to happen to them."

▼ ▼ ▼

They crept up to the garage, opened the door, ducked under, closed it, and without a word threw themselves at each other, staggering across the floor locked together

118

like exhausted dancers. When they fell on the couch, another of its legs broke, but it didn't matter. They were kissing like there was no tomorrow. Real kisses, fierce ones, kisses that bruised, kisses that sucked the oxygen out of the air—a delirium of kissing.

Finally Tess scrambled toward the slantier end of the couch. "Gabriel, we've got to stop."

Light came in one long flat plane at the top of the partly sprung door. He could see her black T-shirt bunched up under her arms. He reached for her. "Tess . . . ," he began.

She jumped up and took two quick steps.

"I wasn't going to do anything," he assured her.

"It's not you I'm worried about." She shook her head vigorously, then slapped herself lightly a couple of times on the cheeks.

He thought for a second. "So you liked it, too?"

"Are you kidding?" She tugged at the neck of her T-shirt. "It was great, but I'm not going to keep even one childlike quality kissing like that."

Gabriel felt one of his front teeth gingerly and grinned. "You can have all my childlike qualities, if you want. I'm through with them."

She took a step toward him. "So you're not mad?"

"No, I don't think so."

"And we can still do stuff together, can't we? Like go places on the bus and make movies and everything?"

"Sure, of course we can." Then he stood up and tried his legs, as if he'd been in traction for six weeks. "I'll be fine. I'm fine now."

"We're friends, right? Good friends. And we don't want to ruin that with, you know . . ."

He stepped up beside her. "It was just so great."

She tugged at him. "Don't talk about it. C'mon. We gotta get out of here."

When there was nobody in the courtyard, Tess asked, "Do I look okay?" Nervously she stroked her hair straight up again. "Different or anything?"

"Your lips are kind of red."

"Oh, man." She patted them like she was fluffing up pillows.

"You have great lips," Gabriel said.

"Don't talk like that, Gabriel. Even talking about it makes me feel funny."

Gabriel glanced toward the picture windows above them. "Funny how? Mad again?"

"No," she whispered, "not mad at all. Just funny." She put her palm on her stomach. "All over." She took his hand then and tugged. "So c'mon. Let's go on upstairs and watch a video or something. But if Mom's home, act natural."

Gabriel grinned. "What if this *is* natural?"

▼ ▼ ▼

Next morning they walked all the way to the bus stop without saying one word. Then they sat beside each other silently. Tess looked as inscrutable as those Mayans painted on the theater walls.

Gabriel sighed a couple of times. Then he coughed. Nothing. So he linked his fingers and played This-is-the-church-and-this-is-the-steeple, silently revealing the same bald congregation again and again.

Finally he looked straight at her and said, "You said yesterday you weren't mad."

"I'm sorry," she said, sliding halfway down the bench

120

to meet him. "That stuff, what we did, you know, upset me more than I thought it would."

"Me, too, probably. I've never done anything like that before."

"In a garage, you mean?"

"Anywhere."

She turned to him, then brushed some invisible dirt off his bare forearm. "You mean you never even kissed anybody before?"

"Not like that. Have you?"

"Gosh, no, but I thought that boys would have . . . you know."

He shook his head and shrugged. "Jocks have, maybe. Or guys who are really cute."

"I think you're really cute."

"If you were Pinnochio, a car would be running over your nose about now."

Tess laughed out loud. "Had you kissed a lot? Before this, I mean."

He shook his head. "Only at parties, a little. Did you?"

"Last year at school this guy wouldn't leave me alone until I did, so I let him, but it was stupid. He smelled like cat food."

"Did you ever practice kissing?" Gabriel asked.

"By myself? Sure, on my pillow."

"Me, too. And I kissed a wall once. These friends of my dad have like velour wallpaper in their rec room, and I kissed that. I guess I thought it seemed more human or something, but it was like kissing a caterpillar."

Tess held up one hand and showed him. "Did you ever make your thumb and index finger like lips and do that?"

Gabriel nodded vigorously. "Sure. I even washed my

hand in real hot water once and then kissed it because I kept hearing about hot lips. That was really stupid. Did you ever kiss a mirror?"

"Uh-huh. It was cold." Tess sat up and faced him. "But that's nothing. A girl at school kisses her dog. I saw her. Yuck."

"Well, a guy at my school kissed baloney. He'd take it out of his sandwich and, you know, fold it to make little thin lips and then kiss it real soft at first and then get turned on and stick his tongue in there."

When Tess finished giggling, she snuggled closer to Gabriel, leaning so their foreheads touched. "I never thought I'd like to do that," she said softly, "with tongues, I mean. But then we did it, and it's not weird at all."

"Gosh, no. It was great."

As Tess nodded in agreement, she stretched, nonchalantly eyeing the traffic. "You know the only thing I wish we'd done different yesterday?"

"Started earlier? Like at dawn?"

"No, I wish we'd filmed it for *Mondo Tess*. God, it was my first really passionate embrace. And now it's gone forever."

They watched the cars again—some big and stern like parents, some little and all over the place like kids who'd had too much candy.

Tess glanced past Gabriel. "Here comes the bus," she said. "I guess we ought to get on."

"You know," Gabriel said, sounding thoughtful. "There's something we could do about yesterday and *Mondo Tess* and all that."

"Really?"

"Sure. We could recreate it for, you know, art's sake."

"Recreate kissing?"

"Uh-huh."

"You mean fake it?"

He looked at her. "I could probably pretend to like it if you could."

She licked her lips as the bus pulled up and the big doors hissed open. Pretty soon the driver glared out at them.

"Hey, are you kids getting on or not?"

▼ ▼ ▼

It was warm and dark inside the garage. Gabriel crossed to the familiar couch, unzipped his sweatshirt, and hung it over the handlebars of Tess's old bike.

Tess balanced the camcorder on some stacked cartons. Then she went behind them and sighted through the lens.

"The light's bad," she said.

Gabriel looked at the bare bulb overhead; black friction tape hung from the bare wires.

"We could turn this on, I guess."

"If we don't, we'll look like two lumps."

"Okay." Gabriel's hands felt huge all of a sudden. Wherever he put them—on both knees, in his lap, stretched out along the tilted sofa—they felt big as shoe boxes.

"Will you get it for me?" Tess asked.

"Huh?"

"The light."

"Oh, yeah."

When the light went on, Gabriel squinted. God, things looked shabby—the couch had big stains shaped like Florida and Idaho. Along one wall half a dozen dresses hung from a sagging wire, their long sleeves looking withered and creepy.

"Sit down, okay?" said Tess. "I'll turn this on and come slinking into the frame."

Gabriel's stomach was turning sour on him, and he swallowed before he said, "You didn't slink yesterday. It just happened, like spontaneous combustion."

"Okay, okay. So I'll explode into the frame."

Gabriel sank onto the nubby couch, avoiding the long stain.

"Move this way." Tess waved him left.

He scooted a little.

"Too much!"

"God, Tess. Make up your mind!"

She let her finger rest on the *auto* button. "Ready?"

"I guess."

Tess darted out from behind the cartons, plopped down beside him, and put her face right up against his. He could see her roll one eye toward the lens as both arms went around him.

"Ouch!" he said. "You poked me in the ear."

"Don't rub it!"

"Well, it hurts."

"This is not about your first wound, okay? It's about my first passionate kiss, so let's kiss."

Gabriel tried. Her lips were tight, like the seam on a softball. "You opened your mouth yesterday."

"Okay." And it flew open.

"I meant," he said, talking right down her throat like a doctor, "when we were kissing." He leaned back and wiped the tip of his nose dry.

"Don't stop. I'm just nervous. I can edit this part out."

A little of yesterday came back then, like an accident victim regaining consciousness. Her arms tightened around him.

"Did we hug or just kiss?" Tess whispered.

"I don't remember exactly, but . . ."

"We'd better hug, too. I'm pretty sure we hugged."

Gabriel stared over her shoulder. In one corner stood a tall flag, the kind everyone in Bradleyville had for July Fourth and Memorial Day. For some reason, Gabriel felt unpatriotic.

"With more ardor now, okay?" She glanced at the camera, then back at Gabriel. "Do you know what *ardor* means?"

"I'm not stupid, Tess. I know just about as many words as you do; I just don't show off about it all the time."

Tess pulled away. "What's wrong?"

"I don't know. I feel funny, not right somehow."

She looked toward the camera. "I guess I've got enough, anyway."

Gabriel's face got hot. His throat started to feel thick. "Who's going to see this stupid thing?"

"Well, whoever sees *Mondo Tess*."

"Well, it's stupid."

Tess slid off the couch and touched the *off* button. It was a lot quieter without the whirr of the camcorder.

"Stupid or not, Gabriel, it's what happened. And *Mondo Tess* is about what happened to me."

"But it's not what happened; it was staged and phony. And it's not just about you. It's about me, too." Gabriel stood up. "So I don't want people seeing this. I look stupid." He glared at her. "I can just see you a couple of years from now showing it to some other guy and laughing."

"What other guy?"

"A boyfriend. A real boyfriend. Not just a prop."

Tess opened her hands to show her innocence. "I would never do that. Never."

"Well, you'd show it to a class, then. At film school. You said so. And I don't want a whole class laughing at me, either."

"God, Gabriel." She reached for his arm, but he jerked away. "I won't show it if you don't want me to. I'll destroy the film. You can watch me."

He gritted his teeth—half ready to bawl, half ready to yell at her. "I thought coming back here was just an excuse." He glared at her accusingly. "It was for *me*. I never thought that you'd do it—set up the camcorder, I mean."

Tess glanced toward her camera.

"And no!" Gabriel yelled. "You can't film this argument, either."

"I wasn't thinking about that. Honest. I was trying to get things straight in my head. Things I wanted to say." One hand raked her hair. She was breathing fast and shallow, like a cat.

Pretty soon, she stepped right up to Gabriel. "Look, I wanted to come back, too, okay? I did. Maybe I wanted the footage, but I wanted to kiss you more." Her hands closed around one arm. "It was an excuse for me, too."

"It sure didn't feel like it. It was like kissing a Barbie doll."

"You've kissed a Barbie doll?"

"Don't change the subject. I mean it wasn't like yesterday at all. It made me feel creepy."

"I know, I know. Me, too. And I apologize. Maybe I was just trying to keep from getting so excited again. Anyway, I'm sorry."

Gabriel rubbed his jaw. His face was dry and hot. "Well, I wish you would've just told me."

"But I didn't know. I wasn't as honest as you, okay? But I know now, and I'm sorry."

He looked at her utterly sincere face. "Okay, okay."

"And I won't use the film. We'll burn it together."

"Good."

Tess slumped onto the couch beside him, squinting up. "Maybe I'll just burn everything," she said through clenched teeth. "Ever since the other day I've been thinking maybe *Mondo Tess* is just this phony bunch of baloney, anyway."

Gabriel straightened his clothes. "What other day? Yesterday?"

"No, with Mr. Palmer, when you were really thinking about the animals and all and how you felt. And then you went ahead and marched."

"Right. So?"

"So what was I doing?" She looked right at him. "Using you and everybody else for *my* movie. So *I* could look good or interesting or special." She scowled toward the piled cartons that held her camcorder. "I mean, God, what if somebody caught on fire or something and I was there? Would I put him out or just say, 'Oh, cool. This'll look good in *my* life story'?"

Gabriel stood up and tucked his blue shirt in. "Look," he said with a tentative grin, "except for today, I think

Mondo Tess is a cool idea, and I don't think you're dishonest or anything."

Tess looked as if she might lose it. She bit her lower lip hard, like one of the soldiers in *From Here to Eternity* when he got shot.

She tugged at Gabriel's hand, and when he sat down again she said, "You're really a nice guy."

He patted her arm. "You're easy to be nice to."

"Do you want a hug?" she asked.

"Sure."

They'd barely put their arms around each other when the door flew open and sunlight charged into the garage. All Gabriel could make out was a luminous shape.

Tess scrambled for her camera. "Aliens!" she screamed.

"Not quite," Mona said, stepping inside.

"Oh, man." Gabriel tried to sit up straight like a good boy.

Mona had her arms crossed. "What do you two think you're doing?" she demanded.

Gabriel tried to catch Tess's eye, but she was tugging at her clothes.

"Nothing," he croaked.

"It hardly looks like nothing to me." Mona's voice sounded torn around the edges. "I thought you were going to the beach."

"Uh, we changed our minds." Tess seemed to be talking to her knees.

"Obviously."

"It was too hot for the beach."

Mona looked around. "Hotter than this place?"

Tess snapped, "I really hate it when you spy on me."

128

"Nobody's spying, just suspicious. I saw you guys sneaking back from the bus stop." Mona uncrossed her arms. "This all started that day you couldn't wait to put the signs away, didn't it?"

Tess stood up and retrieved her camera. "Mom, we weren't doing anything!"

"Really? You lied about where you were going and what you were going to do. Why should I believe you now?"

"Because it's true." Gabriel stood beside Tess. "Nothing was gonna happen." He pointed at the camera. "We were working on *Mondo Tess*."

Mona put both hands to her face for a second. "Gabriel, every high school kid who ever got pregnant said nothing was going to happen."

Gabriel looked at Tess. "She thought we were doing *that?*" Then he stared at her mother. "We weren't doing that."

"You might not mean to," Mona pointed out, "but things get out of control."

"Just kissing?" Tess asked.

"Especially kissing." Mona looked around. "Especially kissing in a garage in the dark on a bed."

"The light's on," Tess corrected her. "And it's a couch."

Mona waved her hands as if she were doing some halfhearted cheer. "Oh, well, then there's nothing to worry about. A couch is a surefire birth control device. Nobody ever got pregnant on a couch."

Tess said deliberately, "Mom, we're sorry. And I know it looks bad, but it's not. I mean it wasn't. What you saw was just like an innocent hug. We'd had an argument, and it was to show everything was okay. Right, Gabriel?"

Gabriel nodded. "Right."

"And we'd really been working on *Mondo Tess*. Right, Gabriel?"

"Right."

Tess hoisted her camera. "Mom, I could show you the rough cut. It's not what you think at all; it's kind of pitiful."

Mona uncrossed her arms so she could rub both temples. Then she sighed. "All right. But I want you guys to make movies in the sun from now on."

They chanted in unison, "Yes, ma'am."

Mona peered into the gloom. "That stupid couch. Desi bought that when we didn't have two dimes to rub together. He said he thought we'd feel better if we had nice things around us."

"Did you feel better?" Tess asked tentatively.

"A little. Your dad could be thoughtful; he still can be."

"So when you and Dad—"

"C'mon, Tess. I'm not that easy to distract." Mona held out a hand to her daughter. "We need to have a little talk. Woman stuff."

"Aw, Mom. We had that talk!"

"Well, we're gonna have it again." She turned to Gabriel. "And I think you ought to go upstairs and wait for your dad."

▼ ▼ ▼

A few hours later, as Sumner paced the kitchen, Gabriel tried to figure out how mad his father was. Sumner seemed different, more concentrated.

Gabriel kept glancing at his dad's pocket, actually hoping Timmy would make an appearance. Instead, Sumner grabbed a diet root beer and rolled it between his palms thoughtfully.

"Sit down," he said finally.

"I'm okay."

"Well, I'm not, and I want you to sit down."

Gabriel, surprised, sank into one of the black chairs.

Sumner chose his words slowly at first, as if he were picking out Scrabble tiles. "I'm very upset with you. And whatever Mona decides to do is fine with me. If Tess is grounded, you are, too. And for however long."

Gabriel looked down at his jeans. "Okay."

"It's not that I can't make my own decisions about your behavior; I can. But I'm at work, and Mona's here. What she says goes, understood?"

"Yes, sir."

Sumner sat down across from his son. "Now, don't misunderstand this."

"I'm not. I know you're mad."

Sumner frowned and shook his head. "I mean don't misunderstand what I'm *about* to say. Don't think I'm condoning some macho-crap, all right?"

Gabriel squinted. "What macho-crap?"

"Scoring with girls or whatever it's called now."

"I didn't score with Tess. We were just kissing."

Sumner plunged ahead. "And when we get back to Bradleyville, if I ever hear of you bragging about this or adding up your conquests or anything like that, we're going to have another one of these talks, and it's not going to be so civil."

Gabriel just stared. This wasn't the Dad he was used to at all.

"Anyway," Sumner said, setting down the root beer with a thunk, "here's what else I want to say—I'm glad you can be comfortable with girls."

Comfortable. Gabriel just stared at his dad.

"I'm not condoning the way you lied about what you and Tess were up to, and I'm certainly not pleased at coming home from work to hear the two of you have been hiding in a garage." He held up one palm like a traffic cop, deflecting anything Gabriel might say. "On the other hand, I was never in a garage or anyplace else with a girl when I was fourteen or eighteen or twenty-two. I couldn't have been. I was too shy and afraid." He squeezed the empty can, making a little dent that immediately popped right back out. "I had friends who were girls, but no girlfriends, if you know what I mean. I was never one of the guys. I was happier planning things or getting there early and decorating or cleaning up afterward."

Sumner smoothed his fine hair. "There was one kissing game once that I couldn't avoid, so I went into the closet with JoAnn Potter, got scared, and peed in my pants."

Gabriel couldn't look directly at his father. "I heard that story."

"Everyone in town's heard that story. It's almost Ozark folklore by now." Sumner put both index fingers to his temples and rubbed.

Gabriel almost leaned across the table and took his father's hand or at least touched his shirt. Instead, he grabbed the saltshaker and tried to balance it on the pepper shaker.

"But you and Mom got married," he said finally.

Sumner picked up the empty can again and pressed,

this time with both hands. It bent in a little and stayed bent.

"That was a lot later. We were grown-ups. And if today is any indication, you're not too many years away from understanding what it means to be grown up."

Gabriel sat back and gingerly felt his tall flat-top. Then he glanced at Timmy. "Tess says all great artists keep their childlike qualities even when they get older. You did."

Sumner snatched the puppet, smoothed his fur, and tucked him away in one pocket. "My childlike quality, huh?" He rolled his eyes toward the ceiling. "I don't know whether to laugh or cry at that one."

Gabriel leaned across the table. "God, Dad—"

"Do you know what I want to do?" Sumner said suddenly. "Eat about twenty pounds of cookies. I know I should want a drink, but I want cookies instead."

Gabriel just stared.

"Of course, then my childlike quality and I will gain about seventeen pounds." He hitched up his pants and suddenly asked Gabriel, "Wanna go for a ride?"

"Where?" he answered cautiously.

"Down to that market we went to our very first night here. Mrs. Maxwell's Ranch Market, remember? Let's go down there, and I'll just *look* at the cookies. This is L.A. I'm sure I'm not the only cookie voyeur in town. And then if I just can't stand it, you'll be along to carry the double-fudge delights. You game?"

"Sure," Gabriel said, standing up. "Friends don't let friends drive stuffed."

When Mona pulled into the Venice Beach parking lot, Gabriel and Tess shot out of the car ahead of everyone else.

"God!" Tess said, spinning around with her arms out. "How long have we been cooped up?"

"A week," Gabriel replied, "but I kind of liked watching videos with you all day, and so far your dad's movie is the funniest."

"It was okay, I guess." Tess took his hand and started down the wide, crowded sidewalk flanked by T-shirt shops, racks of sunglasses, places to rent skates, and a hundred fast food stands.

Gabriel looked over his shoulder, finding the others by picking out Cassandra's muumuu. "I'm just sorry Mr. Palmer had to get depressed so we could get un-grounded."

"They'll catch up in a minute," Tess assured him. "Then we'll make him feel better."

Gabriel liked the way she touched him all the time now, especially the easy way her arm went around his waist. He was like the guys he'd seen in Bradleyville, the ones who also had girlfriends.

As Mona and Sumner struggled toward them with a basket of food, the kids watched a beefy guy in red shorts and a top hat who juggled chainsaws.

"Not like Bradleyville, huh?" Tess asked above the kennel-like snarl of the tiny engines.

Gabriel shrugged. "It's not really stuff like this that makes L.A. different, you know? Guys like these are at the Riverfront in St. Louis or Six Flags. It's the regular people and the way they are—they're like more generous or something."

Tess stood on her tiptoes to locate Mr. Palmer. Then she said, "Those guys your dad works for don't sound so generous."

"Well, the people that I know are."

The six of them had just started down the sidewalk, past the blue wall with the mural of a smoking volcano and a giant wave, when a blond couple rounded a corner. Both wore tiny white bathing suits and white clogs. Her hair was piled straight up, and his goatee pointed straight down.

"I looked like that in a former life," Cassandra said between sips at her thermos.

"Which one?" Gabriel asked.

"Which life?"

"No, which person?"

She closed both eyes, concentrated, then frowned. "Both. That was a bad life."

Tess glided up beside Mr. Palmer. "Tell me about all the body stuff again, Mr. Palmer, okay? What'd you call it—physical culture, right?"

He blinked and used both hands to rub his face. "Well,

135

we like to stress that narcissism is an unfortunate by-product of some aspects of the natural life."

She patted the back of his hand briskly. "What else? C'mon. I'm interested."

"Well, Theresa, at their best, people love themselves because of their likeness to what's divine and not because they're more physically attractive than the next fellow." He plucked at the neck of his cotton pullover. "Sunny was never a classic beauty, and she would have laughed at the idea of spending hours in a gymnasium. But she was full of healthful vitality and"—his fingers tightened on the mesh bag he carried—"she had so much inner beauty that everyone loved her. Everyone."

When he started to quiver, Gabriel patted him on the back.

Mr. Palmer plunged ahead. "When she chose me, I thought I was the luckiest man in the world." He sniffed two or three times and put one hand to his chest. "When she said yes that day so many years ago, I could feel the life force, which had been partly dormant, expand and fill every cell of my body."

Mona waited a bit, then said softly, "C'mon, or they'll use up all the sun."

Tess and Gabriel took a turn lugging the wicker basket. It was clumsy, and they fell behind the others. Edging around a five-man bongo recital, they saw Sumner waiting for them.

"You know," Tess said, "your dad looks pretty hip these days."

Gabriel looked his father over. "He reminds me of your dad now."

"No way," Tess protested.

"Are you kidding? A big blousy shirt and big blousy pants with little cuffs."

"Well, then they look better on him than on my dad."

It was Gabriel's turn. "No way," he said with a smile.

They dropped the basket and took a Coke from Mona, who'd stopped in the shade of a purple awning.

"Hide your eyes, Mr. Palmer," Tess teased. "You don't want to see all this sugar and caffeine."

He played along, raising his hand to his face, but immediately letting it fall away wearily and, with it, his smile.

Gabriel noticed that every line on Mr. Palmer's face curved down: from the big creases—shaped like croquet wickets—that ran across his brow and down both cheeks, to the smaller ones beside his nose and mouth, to the tiny ones hardly larger than staples. All arcing down like sad faces drawn by kindergarten children.

As a man in a skintight electric blue bodysuit went by walking on his hands, Gabriel asked Mr. Palmer, "Has it changed a lot?"

"It's been a few years since we've"—he caught himself—"since *I've* been here. And it's always been fantastic in its own way." Then as some tough-looking kids wearing only rally caps, shredded jeans, and skates roared past, yelling at people to get out of their way, Mr. Palmer added, "Perhaps a little less loving energy. But then, we aren't at the beach yet, either. Not really."

Gabriel looked to his left, past the paddleboard courts, to the sand. There were a few isolated people: one resembled the *X* on a treasure map; another curled up catlike; two more lay rigidly side by side like people who'd argued and then gone to bed.

Mona tugged at Sumner. "Let's go see if Joan's here today."

"Who's Joan?"

They'd walked a dozen yards when Gabriel looked around, missing Mr. Palmer. He found him watching some weight lifters and in particular one slender blond. She wasn't pumped up like the others. Just lean and tanned.

Gabriel saw Mr. Palmer push the sleeve of his loose white sweater back and examine his own forearm. Then he glanced at the others, their oiled skin glistening.

"Mr. Palmer?" Gabriel slipped up beside him. "Want to find the others?"

"Of course. Yes." He turned half away, then back again. "How old are you, Gabriel?" he asked without looking at him.

"Fourteen. But I'll be fifteen in—"

"Do you need money?" He was facing Gabriel now, his blue eyes focused on him.

"Gee, no. I just had a Coke and—"

"I mean for your future. For your whole life, which is ahead of you. You see, I have money."

"Gosh, Mr. Palmer. I don't think so." He put his hand on the old man's bony shoulder. "Knowing you has been more valuable to me than, you know, money. Shoot, I'm the one who should give *you* something, not the other way around."

Mr. Palmer looked for an instant as if he might cry. Both eyes squeezed shut, and his whole face fisted up.

"You're a very nice young man," he said finally. "Exceptional. Do you know that? It's been such a pleasure to meet you and your charming father."

Gabriel was embarrassed. "C'mon," he said, ducking his head. "Let's go find Tess."

She wasn't that far away, mixed in with a large crowd watching something, but Gabriel couldn't be sure what. He could hear, though, a woman singing the John Lennon song "Give Peace a Chance." Most everybody joined in on the last line or two, then applauded.

As the crowd broke up, Gabriel wormed his way through until he stood between Tess and Mona.

"What's up?" Tess asked.

"I was just talking to Mr. Palmer." Then he took a look. "Wow! Is this Joan?"

"Ms. Jukebox to you, young man," Mona kidded him. "For a buck she'll sing anything."

Joan had transformed herself: she was square like a jukebox, and columns of colored bubbles streamed up and down past the Wurlitzer trademark angled across the painted plywood. Inside, underneath the clear plastic hood, where the turntable would've been, was her head. This she'd painted red and green and topped with a tight silver cap with a golden record attached, something like a graduate's mortarboard.

Her eyes scanned the crowd. "Requests? Requests?"

Cassandra took another sip from her Dick Tracy thermos. "Probably balancing out some heavy mechanical karma."

Mr. Palmer patted his pockets. "Do you know 'I'll Be Seeing You'?"

The green brow wrinkled. "Is that Elton John?"

"Before Elton John," said Mona dryly. "If that's

possible." Then she leaned down and kissed **Mr. Palmer** on the cheek. "No sad songs today, okay?"

"It was Sunny's favorite."

"Maybe later." She tugged at his arm. "C'mon. Let's hit the beach."

In a minute or two, the crowds thinned a little and the vendors got more scarce. Near a set of bathrooms set in a concrete bunker, Cassandra raised one hand.

"Pit stop," she announced. "Won't take a minute."

Everyone put their things down, stretched, and looked around. Not ten yards away, catty-corner from a guy playing a kazoo in front of an empty hat, two tiny penguins marched left, then right, then left again across a stage made by cutting a hole in a refrigerator carton.

Sumner, pretending to be tugged that way, led the others.

"Hi!" piped Timmy.

The other hand puppets stopped, then turned their backs.

"What is this," Timmy asked, "hide-and-seek?"

"Go away," said a deep voice.

Timmy glanced at the spectators, then back. "I know, I know. You're thinking, 'There goes the neighborhood. All those otters know how to do is breed and play on their Slip 'N Slides at all hours.' Well, don't worry. I'm just passing through."

A couple of skaters who'd stopped grinned and nudged each other.

"Go away!" said the cardboard box.

Timmy turned to the small crowd. "Crabby penguins are bad, folks, but not as bad as dolphins. They think they're so smart." He minced around and pitched his voice even higher. "'We can talk to scientists. Our pictures are on all the Greenpeace mail.'"

"Hey, I'm trying to make a buck here," said the box over the crowd's good-natured laughter.

Timmy leaned forward to inspect the penguins. "You guys ever thought of sport clothes?"

The carton scraped on the concrete. "Scram, okay?"

"I'll do better than that," said a gravelly voice from the back of the crowd. "I want you off the beach for good, you fat fruitcake."

Everyone turned. The guys who'd charged past them earlier were back. The leader of the pack—a stocky blond who kept wiping his nose on his leather wristband—had both hands on his hips, and he glared at Sumner defiantly. Behind him, his pals circled noiselessly, all of them wearing the same smirk.

The crowd, like something exploding in slow motion, disintegrated, moving off in every direction, faces averted.

Sumner swallowed, then cleared his throat. "We weren't bothering you."

The blond adjusted his shredded tank top so the right muscles showed. "'We weren't bothering you,'" he mimicked. "'We weren't bothering you.'" Then one hand shot out, and he snarled, "Well, you're wrong. You *are* bothering me. The way you look bothers me, that stupid thing on your hand bothers me, and that little fruity voice bothers me. You dig?"

Gabriel stared at his shoes. Guys like that had always scared him, but they sure weren't being fair. Sumner wasn't hurting anybody.

Suddenly Gabriel found himself stepping forward. He

felt his fists clench and heard himself say, "You guys leave my dad alone. He's a performer, and you're interrupting his performance."

As Tess's camera clicked on, Gabriel felt the whole gang looking at him—not just the stocky leader wearing the skull belt buckle, but the rangy kid in the leather pants, and the weasel-boy with three teeth missing, and the hotshot with an entire shrine to the Virgin Mary tattooed on his chest.

He was the one who asked, "Oh, yeah? And what are you going to do if we don't, *cabrón?*"

Tess, disregarding Mona's protective hands on her shoulders, stepped up beside Gabriel, her camcorder still running. "Look," she said evenly, "I've heard of you guys, and I know we're on your turf, but what's it gonna do to your rep to pop a bunch like this? I mean look at us."

So they did, their eyes resting on everyone in turn. Then they looked at each other as Mr. Palmer suddenly brandished his orange.

"Well?" he demanded. "I abhor violence, but I will not be intimidated. This beach belongs to everyone, do you hear? Not just a gang of ruffians."

The blond kid dug for cigarettes. "Ruffians," he repeated. "Oh, man." He lit a filter tip and let smoke pour out of both nostrils like the dragon in a children's book.

Then he suddenly ground it out under one wheel and snarled, "Let's boogie, guys," and they were gone, all of them bent low, their hair streaming out behind them as if they were carrying urgent messages.

As Mr. Palmer preened, the others glanced around, relieved.

142

Gabriel sighed. "Whew."

"They were just punks," Mona said, and Sumner nodded.

"I read those guys right off," Tess announced. "They weren't going to do anything. They just like to ruin things for other people."

"Follow me," said Mr. Palmer, starting off on his own.

As they picked up their things, a hefty man with a beard rushed out from behind the tall carton. He wore his penguin puppets on both hands like gloves.

"What do you say you come back in an hour or so and we do this again?" He glanced at the shoe box with a few bills in it. "Split the take, okay? We'll play it the same way—you just come out of the crowd, and I'll pretend to be miffed."

"No, thanks," Sumner said. Then he turned to his friends. "Let's go."

Tess, who'd been watching through her eyepiece, lowered the camera.

"You know," she whispered to Gabriel, "ever since that day in the garage, I think I'm getting a better sense of when to use this and when not to. I think my work's gonna improve, really."

"Wait." The bearded man moved to cut Sumner off. "Why not? It'd be good for both of us."

"Timmy and I are under contract with Oxley Studios. We can't do free-lance work." He wiped at the line of perspiration on his forehead and squared both shoulders. "Now, if you'll excuse us."

They filed down the beach again. Mr. Palmer led the way. Gabriel saw Mona slip her arm through Sumner's and smile up at him. He watched her adjust one of the turquoise earrings that matched her shorts and the woven strands that held her sandals on.

"Speaking of Oxley Studios," she said, "any progress down there?"

Sumner stared down at his espadrilles. "I sure like these shoes," he said.

"Does that mean you don't want to talk about it?"

Sumner shrugged so hard his whole body went up and down. "When I told them that the option runs out next week and I wasn't interested in renewing, all of a sudden they got cozy with me again. They're all petting Timmy and saying, 'Don't you like it out here, little fella?'" Sumner adjusted his cap. "And yesterday the head writer said I was just about the canniest negotiator he'd ever seen." He looked down at his son and let one hand rest on Gabriel's warm shoulder. "They think I'm holding out for something. They think I've got ice water in my veins." He grinned and mopped his high forehead again. "I'm leaving here a legend."

Leaving. Tess looked at Gabriel.

"Did I tell you their last great idea?" Sumner added as they strolled on. "This didn't even come from the guys I work with. This came from the top, meaning some twenty-eight-year-old M.B.A. from Harvard." Sumner stopped, and the others gathered around him. "Guess the name of the character they want to come from Russia and team up with Timmy?"

"Well," Tess began, "if he's Russian . . . Gorby the Goose?"

Mona tried: "Boris the Bear?"

"I know this," Cassandra said. "I just can't think of it right now."

Sumner couldn't help himself. "Igor—" He started laughing.

Tess nudged him. "C'mon. Igor what?"

Sumner started to turn pink and leaned against the concrete wall. "Igor Beaver," he gasped.

When he calmed down—when everyone calmed down—he added, "I was sitting at that round writer's table laughing so hard Timmy flew off."

"And otters hate to fly," Timmy interjected. "A sea cruise, maybe, but . . ."

"Unfortunately I was the only one laughing," Sumner added.

"They didn't get it?" Tess asked.

He nodded vigorously. "I had to explain to them why it was funny. So they said, 'Oh, that won't work, then. Our concept people see him as a sinister beaver wearing a big fur coat and a shoulder holster, not running all over the place.'"

In another twenty yards or so, Mr. Palmer stopped and looked around.

"I think this is it," he said.

Gabriel scanned the sand. Nobody seemed to have much on, but nobody looked buck naked, either.

"This is clothing-optional out here, right?" Gabriel whispered to Tess. "You promised."

"Relax. The really, really nude beaches are like away from civilization. This one is just do-your-own-thing. Or used to be, anyway."

"Did you ever take all your clothes off when you came here?"

"Are you kidding?"

"Did everybody else?"

145

"Not everybody. And they lay down first and were pretty cool about it all. I mean nobody was prancing around in his birthday suit, not really. Anyway, I was about four years old. I was used to Mr. and Mrs. Palmer, so it was no big deal. The main thing I remember is they let me go stand by the ocean by myself. That was a rush."

Mr. Palmer held up one hand, and the little caravan stopped. He looked puzzled. "Perhaps more west?" he said.

"You go west, young man." Cassandra was panting. "I'm staying here."

"Let's do settle here," Mona said. "If it's just awful, we'll move."

Gabriel glanced around. There weren't very many people, certainly not the yards and yards of bare skin he'd been both hoping for and afraid of. A few women had untied their tops and folded them strategically across their breasts. Someone had a boom box cranked up, and whatever nudist music was, he wasn't playing it.

Everyone but Cassandra, who was wearing a muumuu with Holstein cows on it, slipped out of their clothes to reveal bathing suits. Mona's was turquoise and cut very high on her legs. Sumner had new black trunks, not Speedos but somewhere between those and his original baggy drawers with palm trees on them. He'd lost his snowman's pallor and was now the color of lightly toasted Wonder bread. Mr. Palmer's suit, though, was very peculiar, like a sock held up with thread.

"I don't think this is it." He frowned at the music. "I'll ask around. Why, I used to know half the people on this beach."

Everyone watched him walk away. His back was mottled and cured by the sun. Once he lost his balance, and Mona took an involuntary step forward.

"He's slowed down so much recently," she said to no one in particular. "Maybe I should have picked a different beach."

"He chose it," Cassandra said, opening up a canvas chair, plopping in it, and adjusting her Dodgers cap. "Don't blame yourself." She sounded matter-of-fact and curt.

"I know, but this is the first time he's been back to Venice since Sunny died."

"She didn't die down here, did she?" Gabriel asked.

"No," Mona assured him. "And for what it's worth, it was quick. She didn't suffer."

"Aneurysm," Cassandra said.

Gabriel looked up at his father, who was adjusting a black cap with ZOOM written on the front. "Like Mom's dad," he said.

"Well, this is fun," Tess said. "'What'd you guys do at the beach, make out and pig on junk food?' 'Nah, we almost got in a fight. Then we put on Sun Block 9000 and talked about who was dead.'"

Cassandra raised her thermos. "I'll drink to that."

Tess leered at her mom. "C'mon, Gabriel, we've seen Muscle Beach. Let's go look for Kissing Beach."

"They never forget, do they?" Mona said to Sumner with a long-suffering grin. "They're like elephants."

Timmy piped, "Back at the pond a lot of young otters sneak into the old hollow log and come out with their fur messed up, but it's just high spirits." He turned his shiny eyes toward them. "They're good kids, Mona."

"Thanks," said Tess, giving his white palm a slap.

"Well," said Mona, "I'll leave a tuna sandwich out in the sun, sweetheart. Just for you."

As they trudged toward the water, Gabriel said, "I'm going to miss your mom, too."

"I know." Tess looked solemn for a second or two; then she shoved Gabriel and took off running. "Race you to the ocean!"

When he pulled up beside her panting, he was stunned by the Pacific. By its size and color—limitless and green-blue. By its muscle—it tugged at his bare feet in the deep sand. And by its sound—a low throat-clearing rumble followed by a slapping boom, then a hiss.

"You've never seen it before, have you?" Tess asked.

Gabriel shook his head. "Not this close. Dad and I drove up the Pacific Coast Highway one day, but we didn't get out or anything." He walked a few steps and felt the damp sand. "It makes me think about stuff from science class—gravity and all that. I still don't understand exactly why the water doesn't run out into space."

They sat down together, his left leg against her right one. Some kids a few years older than them scrambled in through the shore break. A woman in her thirties let her toddler crawl around on his hands and knees. An older couple, both in rolled up white pants like an ad for early retirement, passed hand in hand.

Gabriel pointed over his shoulder. "When those kids who just ran past get married, they'll have a kid of their own like that one there. And then they'll get older"—he glanced to his right—"like those people. And then like Mr. Palmer."

Tess picked up Gabriel's hand and wove her fingers through his.

"Are you afraid of dying?" she asked.

Gabriel poked the sand with a Popsicle stick he'd found. "Sure, I guess. Especially if it hurts." He turned to her. "Are you?"

"Mr. Palmer says it's the most natural thing in the world. He says that we're all just tiny versions of everything."

Gabriel shook his head. "I don't get it."

"Well, just that our breath is like the wind or our blood is like a river. We're like the world, then, right? It gets old and changes; we get old and change, and eventually we just go out like stars go out."

"We're still getting light from stars that died a long time ago. Did you know that?"

"Yeah, and if you were a really, really nice person or an artist or something, people would get light from you after you're gone, right? From things you did and left behind. Like from my movies and the little kids your dad teaches who turn out nice." She made a capital *T* in the sand. "Anyway, Mr. Palmer's not afraid. And I might not be, either. So much, anyway."

Gabriel leaned into her. "Can our folks see us?"

"Probably. Why?"

"My lips are lonely."

She put her forehead against his. "Were they right, though? Were we gonna get in trouble?"

"I don't know. I got pretty excited. It was like being drunk or something."

"I know girls at school who said they just got, you

know, carried away. And I'd think, 'What a bunch of jerks. What a stupid excuse.' But I could have, couldn't you?"

"Yeah." Gabriel's voice was husky.

Tess laughed, rolled over onto her hands and knees, then sprang to her feet. She held out one hand. "Let's go eat."

When they got back to the blanket, everyone was dozing. Cassandra was out cold, snoring lightly, showing all five of her teeth. Sumner lay on his side. Opposite him, knees drawn up the same way, lay Mona. When Tess and Gabriel sat down, their parents stirred.

"A garage washed ashore," Tess said. "We went mad with passion. We couldn't help ourselves."

Mona smiled sleepily and touched her daughter's face. "I love you, Theresa."

Tess fell forward, curling into her mother's arm. "So does that mean I don't have to eat the poison tuna?"

Then everybody but Cassandra reached for the big basket and started to take things out. Gabriel had his mouth full of potato chips when he saw Mr. Palmer. And it was clear he wasn't alone, either. Another man was following, gesturing helplessly.

When Mr. Palmer stalked up to the blanket, his friend followed. He wore the same kind of peculiar and embarrassing swimsuit. And he was old, too. Seventy-five or eighty, with a fringe of long white hair low on his otherwise bald head.

He looked down at everyone and nodded, but kept arguing with Mr. Palmer: "Things change, Pete. If you're smart, you change with them."

Mr. Palmer faced the other man. "Ben, I simply wanted to be nude, and the Gestapo wouldn't let me."

Ben addressed everyone, hands out in that what-can-I-do gesture. "They were not Gestapo. They're the beach police. And if it hadn't been for them, the dope dealers and drug addicts would have taken over the beach. The police make that riffraff toe the line—they can't exclude us just because we're nice. Laws are laws."

"It's absurd." Mr. Palmer's mouth was set. "And as far as the so-called beach police are concerned, I don't need them. I just faced down a gang of thugs. I can take care of myself."

"You haven't been here! You don't know what it was like. Things are pretty good again. All right, a few more restrictions, maybe. But it's almost like it used to be."

"Almost?" Mr. Palmer raised himself on his toes, as though his anger had made him taller. "Is that what I should be satisfied with—almost? We're talking about freedom, Ben. And almost having freedom is tyranny, not 'pretty good.'"

"Pete, take it easy. Calm down. You're gonna have a—"

"I don't want to calm down. I want to be part of nature, free like the animals." He tugged at his tiny suit, struggling out of it. "Here I am!" he shouted. "Arrest me if you will, fascist beach police, threat to society that I obviously am!"

As he stomped away, Mona and Sumner hurried after him. Gabriel was too stunned to move.

Just then Cassandra sat straight up. The jewel in her cap caught the angled sun. "Ahh," she said, turning to Gabriel, "so that's why."

He looked at Tess, then back. "So what's why?"

"Why you're here."

"On the beach?"

"In L.A. At the Harmony Arms."

"So?"

"I can't tell you yet. But soon now, I think."

Gabriel glanced toward Mr. Palmer, who was arguing with the others, resisting any attempt to make him dress.

"Has it got something to do with him?"

Cassandra nodded and upended her thermos into a cup. "All I can say is I'm either going to have to drink more or less, 'cause this isn't going to be easy."

TTTTT

It was barely nine o'clock in the morning, but Gabriel
and Tess were already down by the pool. The sky was all
one color—smooth and gray like the curved sides of an
abandoned quarry—and it was chilly. Gabriel zipped his
sweatshirt as Tess handed him the camcorder.

"I feel bad," she said. "Take a medium-close shot for
Mondo Tess, okay?"

He pointed to the tiny microphone. "Do you want to
say anything?"

She shook her head. Gabriel looked at her over the top
of the camera: there were the flat planes of her cheeks,
those piercing eyes, her spiky hair that was so much her
it was like a monogram.

Then he peered through the viewfinder so he wouldn't
miss anything. Tess was biting her lower lip and swallow-
ing hard. After a few seconds she waved the camera
away.

"Everything's different all of a sudden," she said. "Mr.
Palmer's all weird. You're leaving." She pointed up. "And
what kind of weather is this for August?"

Gabriel moved closer. "Did I tell you he tried to give
me a bunch of money that day at the beach? I mean like
all his money."

"Mr. Palmer did? You're kidding."

153

"He said my whole life was ahead of me."

Tess shivered and rubbed her bare arms. "I didn't know what to do when he started to cry on the way home."

"Me neither. When my dad used to cry after Mom left, I'd just go in the den, but . . . you know, there wasn't enough room in the front seat."

Tess cracked a minismile, then put her face in the crease of his neck.

"It's not only Mr. Palmer I'm sad about," she murmured.

Gabriel looked down at his hands resting comfortably around her waist. Just a few weeks ago, he'd imagined they were as big and clumsy as hooves.

"I know," he said. "Me, too."

"Let me take some shots of you packing, okay? Maybe I'll use it at the end of *The Big Nap*."

"I'm supposed to be packing now. I can't believe our plane's just the day after tomorrow."

Just then a door opened at the top of the stairs. Mona glanced over the railing, waved, and headed their way. She had on the shiny green pants she always wore to ride her Exercycle. Over one shoulder hung an enormous bag with a zipper.

Mona touched each of them lightly before she said, "This could take all afternoon; Toby's not sure. So I called Cassandra, and she's going to be around. In fact, she said it was a perfect day, whatever that means. Anyway, just go over there if you want anything. Sumner could come home early, but I doubt it. He's tying up all the loose ends down at the studio." She scrutinized them both. "You guys okay? You look kind of droopy."

"We're fine."

Gabriel asked, "What are you today?"

"Upset, but at least I'm a human." She pointed. "I've got a little black dress in here. I have to stand at a deskful of bills and wish my husband had had life insurance."

"Don't worry about us," Tess said. "We know the rules."

"Did you see those videos your dad left for you?"

Tess made her eyes cross. "More dailies for *Clan of the Cave Babes*. I can hardly wait."

"There are some others, too. Ones he thought you'd like. At least glance at them, okay? So when he asks I don't have to lie."

Tess nodded.

"Give him a break, Tess," Mona urged. "He's trying."

"All right. I'll look at the tapes."

"I'll make sure she does," Gabriel said, trying to look menacing.

"Oh, have either of you seen Mr. Palmer this morning?"

They shook their heads in unison. "Dad swam by himself," Gabriel said. "He was talking at breakfast about how odd it felt."

Mona frowned. "Cassandra said he was sleeping."

"That thing at the beach was rough on him," said Tess.

"I suppose. And also he was swimming late last night. I got up to go to the bathroom and heard something. It was dark, but I know it was him." She inhaled deeply and let it out with a whoosh. "If you don't see him pretty soon, go over and check, okay?"

Then Mona kissed them both and took off, fishing for her keys as she skirted the pool.

She'd barely disappeared when Cassandra came out of her apartment carrying her roller-blades. She wore a black muumuu and black high tops.

"Hi, guys," she said, sounding—to Gabriel, anyway—a little too casual. Then she sat down on a nearby chaise and began to fiddle with her skates. "Thought I'd do a mile or two. Tone up the old gams."

"You don't have to watch us every minute." Tess sounded edgy. "We're not going anywhere."

"Who's watching anybody? You guys are talking, and I'm exercising. Nobody's watching."

"Did Mona tell you about the garage?" Gabriel asked.

Cassandra looked up. Her face was creased like a dried apple. A dried apple with something on its mind. "What about the garage? Does she want you guys to clean out the garage today?"

Gabriel and Tess exchanged glances. "No, that's okay."

"Good." She put her skates down. "'Cause I've got a little something I want you to help me with. A favor for Mr. Palmer. It won't take very long if we start now."

"If it won't take very long," Gabriel said, "why do we have to start now?"

"Oh, I thought we'd just get it out of the way and have the rest of the day to, you know, relax."

Tess shrugged. "Okay, I guess. What is it?"

Cassandra stood up. "Follow me." She hustled over to the little gate that led out of the pool area. It opened with a creak, and she held it for them. "C'mon."

Gabriel whispered, "Why do I feel like we ought to leave a trail of bread crumbs?"

"Oh, by the way," Cassandra said, "bring that chaise with the wheels on it."

Suspiciously, they each took an arm of the long red-and-white lounge.

"This is for Mr. Palmer?" Tess asked.

"Uh-huh." Cassandra adjusted her muumuu, squaring off the shoulders and neck.

"So he's awake," Gabriel said.

"Uh, not exactly."

"Well, aren't we going to wake him up?"

"Uh, not exactly."

Gabriel stopped. "Were you a parrot in a former life? What's with all this 'not exactly' stuff?"

"Let's go inside and discuss this." Cassandra opened Mr. Palmer's front door with a key. "Just roll that in."

The living room was cool and quiet behind drawn shades. Mr. Palmer's sunburst afghan lay neatly folded on a footstool in front of the reclining chair. A copy of *Vegetarian Times* was open to a pageful of recipes.

Cassandra put a hand on Gabriel's shoulder. "Mr. Palmer wants you kids to do this."

"He wants us to bring pool furniture into his living room?" said Gabriel.

"I meant he wants you to help me."

"Fine," said Tess softly. "We're helping you. The question is—what are we helping you do?"

Cassandra pointed down the hall. "C'mon."

Gabriel put one hand out, and Tess took it. They stood behind Cassandra as she opened the bedroom door. Peering around her, they saw the neatly made bed with its moon quilt and, lying on top of it, Mr. Palmer in his white cotton drawstring pants and pullover.

"We, uh, need that chaise," Cassandra said, glancing toward the living room.

Gabriel took a step back, pulling Tess with him. "What for?"

"To get Mr. Palmer out of here."

Tess swallowed hard. "Why can't he just walk out when he wakes up?"

Cassandra turned. Her hands, hot as a baker's, closed over theirs.

"Because he's left his body."

"Oh, God." Tess's voice broke.

Cassandra leaned toward them. She rolled her eyes toward the bed. "There's nothing to be afraid of. That's merely the container he used in this incarnation."

Gabriel flattened himself against the wall. Tess held his hand so tight it hurt.

"We have to call somebody," he croaked.

"Who?" Cassandra asked.

"The police, I guess."

"Why? There's no crime. He dropped his body very consciously."

"How do you know that?" Tess asked.

"Oh, I was there. I facilitated."

"You helped him?" The question jumped out of Gabriel. He said it again, quieter. "You helped him?"

"I put my arms around him. He wanted to be held. Otherwise he did it completely on his own. It's not like he didn't know it was coming." She smiled. "Then when he passed over, I cleaned up and got things ready."

Gabriel looked down. "My legs feel funny."

"That's natural," Cassandra said. "You'll be fine in a minute. Then we can get that chaise in here."

"I still think we ought to . . . ," Gabriel began. Then, "What do we need a chaise for?"

Tess turned and started for the living room. "I'm calling Mom."

"Wait! Hear me out first. Please."

Tess looked at Gabriel, then came halfway back.

"Mr. Palmer doesn't want to be buried in the conventional way," Cassandra said, "at least not right now. Remember, Tess? He discussed this with all of us not long after Sunny died."

Tess's eyes widened. "You're taking him to the Mojave, aren't you? Like he said he wanted."

Cassandra smiled. "*We're* taking him."

"Taking him to where?" Gabriel asked, looking at Tess.

"He told Mom and Cassandra and me that he wanted his body to be left out in the desert where the sun would just kind of bake him away."

"Is that so much to ask?" Cassandra asked. "Mona said she wouldn't do it, which is her privilege. But later I told him I would if I could." She looked at Gabriel. "When I saw you the first time, I knew it would be all right."

Gabriel pointed into the bedroom, with its celestial ceiling. "You said you had a project for us to help you with. Well, this isn't a project. Macrame is a project, or refinishing a table. This is . . . I don't know what this is. It's screwy. Can't we just call an undertaker?"

Cassandra adjusted her baseball cap, creasing the bill. "Yes, we can, but it's not what he wanted." She pronounced the last few words distinctly.

"But isn't this against the law?"

"There are higher laws, Gabriel. And even if there weren't, who does it hurt?" She looked at them both. "No one. Am I right?"

He looked at Tess. "What do you think?"

"I don't know."

Cassandra pointed toward the dresser. "He left a will and a letter, which I'll mail in a few days. It explains everything without naming names. All he wants is a few days by himself in the Mojave. Then the authorities can do what they like."

"I thought you said he'd passed over? That means his soul or whatever is gone, doesn't it? So what's the difference?"

"Probably not much. But why leave even a little bit of restless energy roaming around wishing for closure?"

Tess was shaking her head. "If my mom knew this was going to happen today, she'd have locked us in the garage with some condoms and a bottle of champagne."

Cassandra was calm. "No one will know. It's two hours there and two hours back. We could stop for lunch in Apple Valley if you want."

Tess laid on the sarcasm. "Oh, lunch. Well, why didn't you say so? I'm in."

"What if somebody shows up while we're taking him to the car?"

Cassandra closed her eyes for a moment. "No, the coast is clear."

Gabriel looked at Tess. "You knew him longer than I did."

Tess turned to the wall and banged her forehead softly against it. "What do *you* think?" she asked without stopping.

"He was a pretty cool old guy."

Tess nodded slowly. Then she took a deep breath and turned toward the living room.

"So let's get going."

Cassandra held up her palm, delighted.

"No high fives, Cassandra," Gabriel said. "Jeez."

A few minutes later, all of them stood by the front door, breathing a little hard. Gabriel and Tess were on either side of the chaise, Cassandra at the head. As they started out, the body slipped. Cassandra grabbed him by the shirt and straightened him out, exactly the way a vice-principal might.

"God, take it easy!" Gabriel cried.

"Did you ever get a check in the mail?" Cassandra asked.

Gabriel eased one of the wheels out the door. "Yeah, sure. Why?"

"And did you keep the envelope?"

"No, but . . ."

She knocked on Mr. Palmer's head with one knuckle. "Well, this is the envelope. The valuable stuff inside is gone. Back to the Universal Bank, you might say."

"Okay, but let's be careful, anyway," Gabriel insisted. "He's still Mr. Palmer to me."

Cassandra smiled. "His spirit is with us now. He's very happy to hear you say that."

"Oh, great!"

Tess reached to close the door. "What happens if we see somebody?"

"We won't. Just go past the pool, back to the driveway, and turn right."

Outside, the courtyard was deserted. Gabriel peered left, then right, then waved the others on. He helped Cassandra keep the lounge moving; Tess took the other end and pulled. Right by the pool, they hit a bump, and Mr. Palmer's arm bounced free. Gabriel picked it up by the sleeve.

"Gee," Cassandra said, "this envelope's getting stiff. Tuck that back in and let's go!"

They paused again behind the Harmony Arms while Tess checked to see if the coast was clear.

"Where now?" she asked.

"To my car."

"Not the Nash."

"Of course."

"What's a Nash?" asked Gabriel.

Tess ignored him. "When was the last time you even started that pile of junk?"

"All will be provided for," Cassandra said serenely, waddling away.

Gabriel, sweating now, leaned forward onto his elbows, found himself inches from Mr. Palmer's hair, and leapt back. Tess kept checking behind her and up and down the driveway.

"This is nuts," she said.

They both jumped when Cassandra's car backfired and, smoking, came shuddering out of the garage.

"See!" she shouted out the window. "I told you so. Purrs like a kitten!"

"What'd she say?" yelled Tess.

"Don't ask."

Cassandra waved. "Bring him up."

Gabriel stared at the smooth-backed little coupe. It was unbelievably filthy, as if it had been pulled out of a lake.

"This is nuts," Tess said again, starting to push. "Or did I just say that?"

All three of them were on the passenger's side, wrestling with the door. Cassandra held Mr. Palmer up. They were just easing him in when Gabriel saw somebody come out onto the black asphalt driveway, look their way, and wave.

"Oh, my God," he said to Tess. "It's Bob, the mailman!"

"Head him off," Cassandra hissed. "We'll handle this."

Tess darted around the car as Bob half-shouted, "I've got Mr. Palmer's vitamins, but there's nobody home."

"Oh, well, I'll take them." Tess pushed her hair back with one sweaty forearm.

"Isn't that him in the car?" Bob asked.

"Push!" said Cassandra, kicking Mr. Palmer behind the knees.

Bob stood on his tiptoes. "What's going on?"

"Oh, he's, uh, practicing." Tess unslung her camera. "He's got a job as an old guy in some commercial about, uh, old guys, and we're just, you know, rehearsing."

Gabriel reached in, grabbed Mr. Palmer under the arm, and flung his hand up and over the top of the car. "Talk to you later, Bob," Gabriel said, trying to sound like Mr. Palmer.

"Sorry," Bob said. "Didn't know you were working." He put the package down beside an oleander bush and walked away.

Seconds later Tess collapsed in the tiny backseat. "My God," she said. "I thought you told us we wouldn't see anybody."

Cassandra put the car into gear and slowly backed up.

163

If possible, the shaking increased. Smoke poured from the back as they reached the street.

"Everything's fine!" Cassandra bellowed.

"Are you kidding? We can't get to the desert in this."

Cassandra shook her head violently, like it was as hard to see as it was to hear. "The car was meant to be this way or it would be different. Everything fits together perfectly to form the fabric we call reality."

Gabriel leaned toward Tess. "Here we are in a Clown-mobile with a dead guy, getting lectures on reality. I'm sure going to be able to write a great essay about my summer vacation."

Tess's eyes widened as Cassandra, wrestling the wheel like she was trying to throw a steer, drifted across the double yellow line. "Are you drunk?" Tess demanded.

Cassandra turned around. "I beg your pardon. I may have some character flaws, but drinking and driving is not one of them."

"Then watch where you're going!"

Gabriel lurched over the seat to try and help her. "And drive in your lane. I think that's a cop car parked over there."

Cassandra peered around Mr. Palmer. "Oh, God, it is. Act natural."

"Under the circumstances, how would that be?"

"Gabriel, reach up under Mr. Palmer's hair. Turn his head toward me. Make his jaw move if you can, like we're having a delightful conversation." Cassandra was very animated for a moment. "Oh, really?" she said to the corpse. "Is that right? How interesting." Then she hissed to Gabriel, "Can you see the police car?"

He peered out the back. "Uh-uh. Too much exhaust."

"Slow down!" Tess demanded.

"I'm trying."

"Well, use the brakes."

"I am using the brakes!"

Gabriel heard the rhythmic thud as the pedal hit the floor. That was soon drowned out by the siren, which was then drowned out by the sound the Nash made as it mowed down a row of newspaper vending machines and crashed into a concrete bus bench.

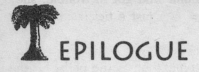 EPILOGUE

The lap pool was wide enough for two people, so Gabriel tried to keep up with his dad but was soon outdistanced. Sumner made a big wallowing turn by himself, then surged up next to his son, who was panting and holding onto the side.

"This is harder than it looks," Gabriel said.

"It just takes getting used to." Sumner pushed a pair of blue-tinted goggles up onto his broad forehead. "We should get you some of these," he said, tapping the plastic lenses. "They really help."

Gabriel let his tongue hang out dramatically. "Seeing isn't the problem, Dad. Breathing is the problem."

Sumner sank into the clear water, then surfaced slowly. "I'm going to miss this," he said.

"Doing your laps?"

His father lay back, letting the water support him. "All of it." Then he reached over and pressed the little Band-Aid on his son's forehead. "Your mom's going to kill me when she finds out you and a corpse were riding in a car that crashed into a bus stop."

"I won't tell her if you won't."

Sumner shook his head. "Whatever my faults as a husband, I never lied to her, and I'm not going to start now."

"Nothing bad happened, anyway, at least not to Tess

and me. Cassandra's the one who got in trouble; she's lucky the cops let her off with just a ticket for driving without a license."

"Still, I have to tell your mom."

"Well, then I'll tell her with you. She's got to understand Tess and I just did it for Mr. Palmer."

Sumner glanced at the nearest chaise. Lying on a green towel were a watch and a portable phone. Gabriel followed his father's proprietary gaze.

"I want to send something from Missouri back to Mona, because that phone she bought us for a good-bye present is pure California."

"It's cool." Gabriel splashed water on his chest. "Let's do some more laps, okay?"

Sumner nodded, but neither of them moved. At a sound, they both looked across the court, toward the yellow door of Mr. Palmer's apartment, but it was only a single workman in a hard hat, kicking at a pile of two-by-fours. Then they looked at each other a little sheepishly.

"Remember that first night we had dinner at Mona's?" Gabriel asked. "And what Mr. Palmer said about that ball player who might turn out to be selfish because he was so talented? I never forgot that. The people out here always make me think about things. Not like Bradleyville." Gabriel sank in order to cool his shoulders. "And they seem to like me without me having to do anything. That's not like Bradleyville, either."

Sumner glanced up at the sun, the shape and color of a Velveeta cheese snack. Then he reached for his hat.

"I know what you mean," he began. "But for me it's that I don't have to *stop* doing things. Out here, even grown-ups like Timmy."

Gabriel glanced at his dad. He squinted at the limpid water. "You know," he said, "uh, speaking of that. I think maybe being embarrassed about Timmy—*me* being embarrassed, I mean—was just like a habit that I picked up." Gabriel smacked the water and watched the spray. He couldn't make himself look right at his father. "You know, a lot of the people back home remind me of what Tess said about those guys at Venice Beach—they like to ruin things for everybody."

Sumner narrowed one hand and made it do S-curves across the surface. Gabriel knew he was playing otter.

"I, uh," Sumner stammered, "really appreciated it when you stood up to that gang of kids that day, when you said, 'Leave my dad alone.' I just"—he tugged at his goggles and fussed with them—"I just appreciated it—that's all."

Gabriel shrugged. "They were bothering you when you were performing. It was rude."

"Well, I'm grateful."

"You're welcome." Then Gabriel pulled himself out of the water and sat with his feet on the edge of the yellow-and-blue tile ledge. Some drops of water slid off his arm and landed on the heavy blue cover of a bound script Sumner had laid nearby. "At least," he said, wiping away the drops, "getting picked up by the cops didn't ruin some big movie deal for you."

Sumner rolled his eyes. "Mona said somebody from the studio might call me back and want to make *Timmy and the Body Snatchers*. If I live to be a hundred, I'll never understand how this town thinks."

Gabriel glanced toward Tess's apartment. "So it's really

all over, right? No movie, no Timmy pajamas, no nothing."

Sumner nodded. "And maybe it's just as well. I like California, and it's been good for me. But I'm not sure I belong here."

Gabriel got to his feet. He watched the water drip from his black trunks and make patterns on the dry cement. Just then the little phone rang, and Gabriel answered it.

"Mom? Where are you? What are you doing home?"

He listened, watching his dad watch him.

"Tonight. Right . . . five-twenty. Really? Great! Do you want to talk to . . . All right. Bye."

Sumner asked if everything was okay.

"She said Warren was driving her crazy with his schedules, so she just flew home. She'll be at the airport to meet us."

Grinning, Sumner heaved himself out of the pool.

"Funny, isn't it?" said Gabriel.

"What is?" Sumner asked, trying to get to his feet.

Gabriel held out one hand, braced himself, and helped his father up.

"Just that their trip turned out crummy, and ours was so cool."

Sumner held onto his son for a second before he said, "I guess it's time to go. I mean the car's packed and all, but better safe than—"

"I thought I'd swing by Cassandra's. I mean I talked to her a little at dinner last night, but I didn't really say good-bye."

"She kind of grows on you, doesn't she? Guess what

she told me at the beach that day: not to blame myself so much for the divorce. She said Alison has a permanent seven-year itch, and even if I'd strangled grizzly bears bare-handed and made love to her twice a day, she wouldn't have been much more content."

Gabriel, blushing, reached for a towel and dried his face first. "Do you think she says things that are true or just things that we want to hear?"

"Beats me, kiddo."

As the workman kicked something else out of the way, Gabriel looked toward Mr. Palmer's apartment again. "I just keep thinking," he said, "that he's going to come out here and give me an orange. It really feels funny not to go to a funeral or anything."

Sumner shielded his eyes, looking up at his son. "That's the way he wanted it. And by the time he's cremated and Mona and Cassandra take his ashes to the desert, we'll be in school in Missouri."

"Too weird," Gabriel said. Then he watched his father smooth his hair back and slip into the pool again. "Dad? Thanks for showing me that stroke, that butterfly thing."

"My pleasure." Sumner squinted up at him. "Oh, Gabriel! When you go to see Cassandra?"

"Yeah?"

Sumner grinned. "Don't go for a ride with her, okay?"

▼ ▼ ▼

Upstairs, cleaned up and dressed for the flight home, Gabriel stuffed one last pair of jeans into the new canvas satchel his dad had bought for him. He heard the shower go on in his father's bathroom as he headed out the door with his bags.

Outside, the lap pool looked smooth enough to walk on. The air smelled like tomatoes—Mona and Tess making sauce for a dinner they'd eat when he was halfway across the country. It was ten-thirty, so the freeway sounds were intermittent and faint: only a distant hiss like someone in another room combing her long hair a hundred times.

Cassandra was standing in her doorway chatting with a man wearing a red shirt with the collar open. Then he hugged Cassandra briskly, turned, and passed Gabriel without a nod.

"Customer?" he asked her.

"From way back, but I call them clients. Doesn't make it sound so much like I'm selling Avon products."

"I, uh, guess I'm going pretty soon."

Cassandra smiled. "Want to come in?"

Gabriel nodded. "Sure. Why not?"

He put his things down on the brown rug, touching his toe to the new green bag. "I put my leather satchel in the Goodwill bin. I'm pretty sure Mr. Palmer is right about that stuff."

Cassandra grinned. "He's very pleased with you."

"You sound like you've been talking to him."

"Oh, I have."

He looked around. Her apartment was laid out like Mona's, but furnished haphazardly: a beige couch frayed at the corners, two soft chairs with short green slipcovers that looked like hand-me-downs for dumpy twins, and empty root beer cans on the cluttered table with its cotton runner featuring a huge happy rooster. A couple of kitchen chairs were pulled away from the table at an angle.

"I'm not," Cassandra said lightly, "a material girl."

"I guess I was expecting crosses or Buddhas or candles or something."

Cassandra shook her head. "I just chat with my clients. Maybe hold one of their hands, or a ring sometimes. It depends." She pointed to the table. "Want to sit?"

"For a minute. I just came to say good-bye."

"I know."

Cassandra's muumuu had golf clubs on it, all irons with black handles, and she gathered it primly around her legs as she sat across from Gabriel.

"Where do you get those things, anyway?"

"I sew 'em myself. Buy remnants at yardage sales and just knock one out. Takes about thirty minutes. I could make you one for the plane. Guaranteed to get you a row by yourself." She smiled, reached for his hands and folded the right one into hers. She took a deep breath. "Much better," she said without opening her eyes.

"What is?"

"The music of your body. Much more melodic and balanced." She opened her brown eyes. "That's why you came to California and to the Harmony Arms in particular. First time I laid eyes on you, you were all out of whack. Sounded like a bunch of cats crawling up a blackboard. Not now, though."

"I came to the Harmony Arms to get harmonious?"

"Exactly."

"Well, what if we'd lived down the street at the Versailles? Would I have learned French?"

Cassandra smiled. "Trust me on this. I'm never wrong."

Gabriel leaned forward, smiling, but left his hand tucked in hers.

"Cassandra, you're never right. Not about the kid in the raincoat who turned out to be a fireplug, not about taking Mr. Palmer to the car without meeting anybody—nothing."

"Those are just details. Small potatoes." Her eyes opened wide. The ruby on her Dodgers hat glowed like a coil. Her voice was soft, yet it went right inside him. "What I'm never wrong about is the big stuff. How you feel about your father. How you feel about yourself."

Gabriel's free hand flew to his chest. He grunted rather than start crying. "I was just talking to my dad," he stammered. "He's actually pretty cool."

"I know. I was watching."

"Did you see me on the phone? That was Mom. She left Warren in Missoula."

Cassandra smiled mysteriously. "Your parents are very interesting." She squeezed his hand. "*Very*. When I dreamed about your mother, she was riding a motorcycle."

Gabriel corrected her: "Bicycle."

"Whatever. But even while she was riding it, she was looking ahead for the next thing, the next project or passion."

"Sounds like Mom."

"She has all this masculine energy, very restless and hard to please. And then there's your dad; he's just like this holiday snack—so soft and sweet. Much more yin than your mother." Cassandra pressed on his hand. "They're who you get to love this time. Not the parents

173

you think you want, but the ones you've got." She smiled at him. "And thanks to them, you're the one with perfect pitch, absolute balance, the best of both their worlds."

Gabriel shook his head. "I don't understand."

"You get your mother's curiosity and zeal. And you get your dad's sensitivity and creativity. Then mix those things with everything that's unique about you, and you get a perfectly wonderful individual."

Gabriel put one hand to his forehead. "This stuff makes me woozy."

She patted his arm briskly and pushed an open can of soda pop his way. "This really has roots in it," she informed him. "So drink some; it'll ground you."

Gabriel took a tentative sip, then some big swallows. "It's cold!"

Cassandra stood up. "Well, sure. I had it ready. I knew you were coming."

When Cassandra opened the front door for him, Gabriel saw Tess standing by the lap pool talking to an enormous lobster. Its soft satin shell absorbed the weak sunlight. When it spotted him, it waved a claw.

Turning, Gabriel said to Cassandra, "I don't know if I'll ever see you again."

"Then I'll come see you."

He shifted his two bags, balancing them better. "Really?"

"Sure, I'll just leave my body. Astral travel is really fast."

Gabriel pictured her zooming across Kansas in her muumuu. "Right. Well, thanks for everything."

She put her hand out. "It's been a pleasure knowing you."

He let the new bag drop. "Me, too."

Gabriel held her hand firmly, as though he weren't just holding but holding on.

"I don't know whether to believe you or not," he said. "I want to."

Cassandra just smiled.

Gabriel tugged a little. "Will you hug me like you did that other, uh, client?"

"You bet!" She opened her arms, and Gabriel stepped in.

Then he hurried across the courtyard to join Tess and her mom.

"Wu Chi's House of Seafood," Mona explained without being asked.

"You look great." He turned to Tess. "Hi."

Mona glanced at them both. "Well, I'll just scuttle out and say good-bye to Sumner again. I'm late for this shoot already." She took off her big soft head, dodged a bobbing feeler, and tucked everything under her arm so she could kiss Gabriel and wrap one claw around him.

Tess raised her camcorder. "Just in case," she explained, "I need a surrealistic dream sequence."

Before Mona hurried away, she stroked her daughter's hair.

"Let's wait awhile, you know? That thing we were just talking about? Okay?"

When she was a dozen yards away, Tess said, "I told her I wanted to get a job at the mall or something. Just so she wouldn't have to work so hard."

"You have to be sixteen to work, I think."

Tess frowned. "Well, then for sure. I've been kind of selfish."

Just then the wind picked up. Tiny dust devils danced across the piles of dirt, and the palm trees swayed. Tess reached for her camera again and pointed it toward the sky.

"The Santa Anas," she muttered, "make everybody drive faster, drink more, and kiss harder." She panned down to Gabriel. "Elvis Miyata had a funny feeling in his gut. Already one of his friends was taking the big nap. What was going to happen next?" When he didn't say anything, Tess lowered her camera. "You okay? You look a little spaced."

"I guess I was thinking about Cassandra."

"Did she do that thing where she told you something, and then your chest hurt and you wanted to cry?"

Gabriel stopped dead. "Wow, yeah. How'd you know?"

"'Cause I went over there once when I was gonna run away from home. I thought I wanted to borrow money, but I ended up bawling all over her table and then just going back upstairs."

"Is she for real, do you think?"

Tess shrugged. "Cassandra's kind of like that Armenian sandwich we had on Pico Boulevard, remember? You gotta throw away a lot of weird stuff, but what's left is pretty good."

They walked toward the foyer, their arms bumping.

When they were almost to the door, Gabriel stopped. "Tess, I'm really gonna—"

Her hands came up and held his right arm, one hand above the other the way kids hold onto a merry-go-round. She looked right at him. "I know. Me, too. But I don't like to cry at the end, you know? I'd never make a movie like that."

He ducked a little so she could put her forehead against his. "Sure," he said. "Okay."

"Have you got a VCR?" she asked, stepping back.

"Absolutely."

"Then I'll send you *Mondo Tess*."

"Cool, but I'll probably wear the tape out."

Suddenly Tess darted forward, kissed him on the cheek, then quickly swung the camcorder into position and waved toward the street. "You go on. I want a shot of your back. I'll meet you in a minute."

Gabriel waited until she was set, then turned, opened the doors, and stepped through. Outside, Mona was leaning—still holding her head like a football helmet—to kiss his dad. Then she hurried toward her car.

"Wave!" Tess shouted, and Sumner smiled over the top of the silver Cougar.

"Where's Timmy?" she asked.

Gabriel slammed the trunk and held out one hand. Almost immediately Timmy flew over the car. Gabriel caught him, slipped his right hand in, and waved the brown paws wildly.

"That's it!" Tess exclaimed, closing in and raising her free hand with the thumb and forefinger meeting to make a circle. "That's perfect!"

Look for All the Unforgettable Stories by Newbery Honor Author

THE TRUE CONFESSIONS OF CHARLOTTE DOYLE
71475-2/ $3.99 US/ $4.99 Can

NOTHING BUT THE TRUTH
71907-X/ $3.99 US/ $4.99 Can

THE MAN WHO WAS POE
71192-3/ $3.99 US/ $4.99 Can

SOMETHING UPSTAIRS
70853-1/ $3.99 US/ $4.99 Can

And Don't Miss

ROMEO AND JULIET TOGETHER (AND ALIVE!) AT LAST
70525-7/ $3.99 US/ $4.99 Can

S.O.R. LOSERS 69993-1/ $3.99 US / $4.99 Can

WINDCATCHER 71805-7/ $3.99 US/ $4.99 Can

BLUE HERON 72043-4 / $3.99 US/ $4.99 Can

Coming Soon

PUNCH WITH JUDY 72253-4 / $3.99 US / $4.99 Can

SPINE-TINGLING SUSPENSE FROM AVON FLARE

NICOLE DAVIDSON

THE STALKER	76645-0/ $3.50 US/ $4.50 Can
CRASH COURSE	75964-0/ $3.50 US/ $4.25 Can
WINTERKILL	75965-9/ $3.99 US/ $4.99 Can
DEMON'S BEACH	76644-2/ $3.50 US/ $4.25 Can
FAN MAIL	76995-6/ $3.50 US/ $4.50 Can
SURPRISE PARTY	76996-4/ $3.50 US/ $4.50 Can
NIGHT TERRORS	72243-7/ $3.99 US/ $4.99 Can

CARMEN ADAMS

THE BAND	77328-7/ $3.99 US/ $4.99 Can

ALANE FERGUSON

OVERKILL	72167-8/ $3.99 US/ $4.99 Can
SHOW ME THE EVIDENCE	
	70962-7/ $3.99 US/ $4.99 Can

⇛TERRIFYING TALES OF⇚
SPINE-TINGLING SUSPENSE

THE MAN WHO WAS POE   Avi
                       71192-3/ $3.99 US/ $4.99 Can

DYING TO KNOW   Jeff Hammer
                       76143-2/ $3.50 US/ $4.50 Can

NIGHT CRIES   Barbara Steiner
                       76990-5/ $3.50 US/ $4.25 Can

CHAIN LETTER   Christopher Pike
                       89968-X/ $3.99 US/ $4.99 Can

THE EXECUTIONER   Jay Bennett
                       79160-9/ $3.99 US/ $4.99 Can

THE LAST LULLABY   Jesse Osburn
                       77317-1/ $3.99 US/ $4.99 Can

THE DREAMSTALKER   Barbara Steiner
                       76611-6/ $3.50 US/ $4.25 Can

Buy these books at your local bookstore or use this coupon for ordering:

Mail to: Avon Books, Dept BP, Box 767, Rte 2, Dresden, TN 38225   C
Please send me the book(s) I have checked above.
❑ My check or money order— no cash or CODs please— for $_____is enclosed
(please add $1.50 to cover postage and handling for each book ordered— Canadian residents
add 7% GST).
❑ Charge my VISA/MC Acct#_____Exp Date_____
Minimum credit card order is two books or $6.00 (please add postage and handling charge of
$1.50 per book — Canadian residents add 7% GST). For faster service, call
1-800-762-0779. Residents of Tennessee, please call 1-800-633-1607. Prices and numbers
are subject to change without notice. Please allow six to eight weeks for delivery.

Name_____
Address_____
City_____State/Zip_____
Telephone No._____ THO 0694